# Lesson Plans

Jamie Jones

ISBN-10: 1-947208-09-8

ISBN-13: 978-1-947208-09-4

2ND EDITION

*For my mom and dad.*

# A Note to the Reader

This edition of Lesson Plans is a re-write. You noticed that I didn't say revised. This book started from a blank word document, not as a revision of a previous work. I changed the way that Monte and Jasmine met, and that changed everything. For the record, the original version was written in 2012 and published in 2014.

# CHAPTER ONE

The Lexus pulled up to the old two-story school building. Jasmine Landers swung open the car door, and her heart raced with the eagerness of beginning a new job. Correction—exploring a new career. She placed one Manolo Blahnik on the lumpy, tarred surface and stared at the structure. Faded grandeur. Finely carved stone and once-sturdy brick, now cracked and weathered. Jasmine loved history. Structures like these made her wonder about all the people who'd passed through in previous decades.

Brookhaven Elementary School in "old" Portsmith, Louisiana, was one of the oldest standing schools according to the human resources department. And it wasn't in the best part of town but, rather, quite the opposite. For a moment, Jasmine channeled Madeleine Kahn from *What's Up, Doc?*

*Is this 459 Dorello Street?*

Jasmine clutched her handbag and stepped out of her car. The air smelled of burnt leaves and a full trash bin. Her heels wobbled on the uneven pavement as she approached the school, and she questioned what she'd gotten herself into.

*My first day as a substitute teacher.*

It had been gnawing at her for a while. Change of lifestyle. Giving back. Something new. Jasmine glanced at the cornerstone of the building, where the year 1916 was carved on cracked limestone. She'd never been to this side of town before. Portsmith, Louisiana boomed with new money, new developments, and a new influx of people. Old Portsmith, the part of town once densely populated, now stood a shell of its former glory.

*So much for something new.*

She clutched her skirt and ascended the stone steps. The door, painted a garish red, stood partially ajar.

In the lobby, a white plastic sign covered with grime simply read OFFICE. Jasmine had arrived early, before her assigned time. Her footsteps echoed in the relatively quiet hallway.

An elderly woman stooped over a desk.

"Good morning. I'm Jasmine Landers."

The lady looked up, as though being disturbed from something, even though the desktop in front of her appeared empty.

"Who are you? A parent?" The old cuss placed a hand on her hip and arched her back.

Jasmine took a deep breath.

*If this is the way the front office speaks to parents, I wonder how they treat the children.*

"I'm here to substitute teach."

The lady looked her up and down and then picked up a weathered two-way radio.

"Wallace!" the crone shouted into the radio.

"Yeah," came back the weary voice through the crackling speaker.

"Unlock twenty-six!"

The lady extended a bony arm, placed the radio on its holder, and went back to looking down at nothing.

"Where am I to go?" Jasmine inquired.

"I just told the custodian to unlock room twenty-six," she snapped without looking up.

Jasmine turned around, only to be barked at again.

"You need to sign in. It's right there in front of you on the counter."

Jasmine's hand trembled as she scribbled her name without so much as a glance up at the receptionist.

*This is how she welcomes a substitute teacher?*

Once in the hallway, she exhaled. A little girl, possibly no more than five, sat on the steps in a pink dress stained with this morning's breakfast. The ribbons in her hair matched her outfit, without the stains.

"Can you tie my shoe?" the girl asked.

"Of course." Jasmine smiled and crouched before the girl, taking hold of her lace.

"I don't know how to tie shoes."

"There, you're all ready for school now. Are you supposed to be waiting on the stairs?"

The little girl shook her head.

"Where are you supposed to be?"

The girl pointed to an open doorway. From the noise level inside, Jasmine guessed the children were waiting in the auditorium for the bell to ring.

"Then you go on ahead. You're all set now."

"Thank you." The girl scurried away.

Jasmine ascended the old stairwell, and she couldn't help but feel she was stepping into the past. Most schools today looked like rows of cellblocks, but this one had a staircase with stone steps and finely carved wooden hand railings.

*Well, here I am.*

She ran a hand along her suit, a pale yellow Chanel. Had she over-dressed? It was her first day, and she wanted to make a good impression. The suit was formfitting and sharp. Jasmine decided she would see how the day went and dress accordingly tomorrow.

The name "Cage" was above the door. Room twenty-six was empty and a bit stuffy. A chalkboard hung from the wall. A real green slate chalkboard, just like something from an old one-room schoolhouse.

*How dated is this school?*

Jasmine opened the attendance book. She counted eleven names.

*Only eleven students. How bad can that be?*

She looked down the list… all boys. Tyrone, DaShon, LeRoy, Lazarus, Dennis, Demetrius, Corey, Pierre, Jordan, Terrance, and Jamal. A glance around the room revealed a dull floor, badly in need of a good waxing. The desks and chairs were chipped and the paint peeled. The windows were dirty and the shades torn in spots.

Jasmine turned around and picked up a piece of chalk. She wrote "Miss Landers" on the board.

A loud bell startled her.

*Here they come.*

There were no instructions, no notes. She'd been told by human resources that Mrs. Cage had been injured, so there'd been no way of anticipating her absence. Something labeled "sub tub" sat on a shelf to the side of the teacher's desk. Jasmine riffled through a bunch of dusty papers. At first blush, it appeared to be a bunch of busy work. This book, that page, this book, that page…they would be bored by that.

"Good morning!"

A robust man with a wide smile filled the doorframe. Handsome was an understatement. He had a bright white grin that lit up his face. Chiseled jaw, deep brown eyes and a deliciously dark complexion caught her attention. Broad shoulders and a barrel chest added to his allure. And his head was shaved smooth.

Athletic coach?

A shiver ran through Jasmine's body. He didn't merely look familiar, she was certain he—

*It's him.*

"I'm Dr. Davis, the principal. Sorry I wasn't here to greet you this morning. I usually like to welcome new teachers to my campus personally."

That deep, masculine voice. Those eyes so focused on her.

He extended his hand, but before Jasmine could approach him, a student brushed by him. The principal stepped back, out of the doorway.

"Good morning, LeRoy."

LeRoy barely mumbled, "Mornin'."

Jasmine still hadn't said a word. Her gaze fixed on the principal, and a tingling sensation crept up her neck. Her ears burned and her stomach fluttered.

*It's definitely him.*

She almost hadn't recognized him with his clothes on. Her lady parts tingled with the memory of his body, the memory of his *everything*.

"LeRoy's been with me a long time. You won't have any problems with him. You can trust me on that one."

LeRoy slouched in his seat.

"Sit up straight, LeRoy. You're a fine young man with a bright future. Be alert and ready to learn today."

A wide grin spread across LeRoy's face.

Jasmine gazed at the principal. He cared about these kids and set a good example for them.

More boys lumbered through the doorway, most of them looking half-asleep. The principal greeted each one of them with a robust welcome, even if they barely responded. After the last one filed in, Davis again extended his hand. "Let's try this again…"

"I'm Jasmine Landers." She placed her hand in his. A wave rushed through her body as his large hand engulfed hers. His firm handshake emphasized his strength. All he'd done was shake her hand, yet her core surged with heat.

"If there's anything I can do for you, Miss Landers, my office door is always open." He released his vise grip and retreated down the hallway with a quick, deliberate stride.

*Why now?*

Those deep almond eyes. His shimmering dark complexion. The unforgettable smile.

*His huge cock.*

He didn't recognize her. He couldn't have. If he had, wouldn't he have said something? No, it wouldn't be appropriate. She couldn't work in the same school as *him*.

And with her core on fire, how could this gig possibly work out? With lust and desire, she'd hardly be able to function with him around.

Chairs scraping against the floor called her attention back to the fact that she was in a classroom.

*And not a hotel room in New Orleans.*

Jasmine turned. Eleven pairs of eyes staring at her. She took a deep breath and smiled.

"I'm Miss Landers." She received nothing resembling a response, either audible or visual. "I'm here to fill in while Mrs. Cage recovers." Jasmine picked up the roll book and faced the class. "When I call your name, raise your hand or say something so I know you're breathing." At least that remark got a few audible grunts.

"Tyrone." A halfhearted gesture to raise his hand, Tyrone still appeared sleepy.

"DaShon."

"'Sup," he responded. At least that was something.

"LeRoy."

"Mornin," LeRoy grumbled, slightly more audible than his earlier greeting to the principal.

"Lazarus."

"Good morning, Miss Landers!" Lazarus shouted, almost sarcastically.

"Dennis." He waved. How had he heard his name with earbuds stuck in his ears?

"Demetrius." He smiled and grunted something inaudible.

"Corey."

"Good morning, ma'am." Corey nodded and grinned.

"Pierre." He nodded.

"Jordan." He was slumped over his desk. Was he awake?

"Hi," he managed to say.

"Terrance."

"Good morning, Miss Landers." He was clearly well-spoken.

"And Jamal."

Jamal made the peace sign and muttered, "'Sup."

Here they were—eleven boys under her supervision. Probably weaned on television and tablets. Now they just needed motivation to learn. Dennis nodded to whatever was coming out of his earbuds.

"Dennis, can you remove those things from your ears please?"

Dennis looked up at her. "Yeah, when you remove that relaxer from your hair."

That elicited roars of laughter from the room. Curiously, she didn't need relaxer. Her hair grew naturally long and full-bodied. Perhaps she'd used too much hairspray.

*Okay, welcome to my new career.*

They were soon talking over one another.

"Pisses me off that I couldn't join the intermediary

school football team this year."

"You too short for the football team!"

"Not gonna stop me!"

"Hey, DaShon, you see him tryna…"

She glanced toward the door, wondering if she could get away with just running to her car and chalking this up to a learning experience. The thought went out of her head as soon as it had entered.

Jasmine had to get them under control or else her day was going to be one big headache.

*How can I rein them?*

"Jordan, will you sit up straight please?"

The boy's head was on his desk. His breathing was deep, as though asleep.

"He does that every day." DaShon shook his head.

Jasmine put her hand on Jordan's shoulder. He didn't stir.

"Jordan…" Jasmine did not get a response.

"He'll come out of it soon enough," DaShon said.

Jasmine nodded and moved on. She should be doing some actual teaching, but until she got them on her side, she couldn't imagine much in the way of education would happen.

Approaching Dennis, she stretched out her hand and said in a very firm voice, "Hand them to me."

Dennis looked up, and his eyes locked with hers.

"Hand them to me now, and I will give them back to you before lunch."

Dennis tried to stare her down, but it didn't work. He slid the earbuds from his ears, handing them to her.

"Thank you." Jasmine deposited them on her desk.

When she turned around, Lazarus was brazenly texting. Jasmine approached him.

"You ain't getting my phone!" he yelled.

"Lower your voice. I didn't ask you for it. Just put it away."

"You ain't getting my phone," Lazarus repeated, his voice dropping a decibel or two. Jasmine sighed. She had to pick her battles if she wanted to get anywhere with this class.

Once she got those few boys settled, the others followed. Before the morning was over, they'd relaxed and she spent the time guiding a group discussion. For now, she kept the talk focused on the students' personal interests both in and outside of school. Might as well keep them engaged discussing their favorite topic—themselves.

The desks were primitive and didn't look all that comfortable. The shelves along the wall were stacked with tattered textbooks probably from a prior generation, and the supply closet had a lock on it. No surprise the kids repeated a grade. The environment hardly seemed conducive to learning.

Did she have the option to take them out of the classroom and do an activity in the library? With the way her day had gone so far, it might be best to stick with the program for now.

Jasmine stepped out of the classroom moments after the boys left for lunch. She grabbed her bag and headed down the steps leading to the main floor. In the short time she'd been with them, she could distinguish many of their personalities. They just never seemed to stop talking.

As she reached the bottom of the stairs, the sound of his voice filtered out from the main office. She gripped the bannister and paused for a moment.

Davis. She hadn't remembered his name. Maybe he'd never told her. His first name began with an M, she remembered that much. It'd been nearly a year. A year in December. That conference down in New Orleans. That one night. One night at the hotel bar and one drink too many.

The heat in her cheeks flared, and her insides tingled. That night had been the most passionate night of her life. A night she'd tried so hard to forget, but it crept back into her consciousness often.

She'd been on her back, legs up high, and he'd pounded into her. All night long. She'd come faster than an express train. And done it again and again. A one-night stand to remember.

If she was going to make it through the day, she had to get him off of her mind. She surely couldn't be on his. He apparently had no memory of her.

*I'll get through this day and not come back.*

How could she come back? Her knees would weaken at the sight of him. Each day she reported to work would be a reminder of the one night. Her insides melted at the memory of what they'd shared together.

After a few deep breaths, she found the teachers' lounge. What she really needed to find was a ladies' room. When did teachers ever have time to pee? The lounge was quiet. In fact, it was empty of people. None of the chattering she expected. And no bathroom. Then again, with only twenty minutes for lunch, one didn't have time for anything but eating.

Jasmine had prepared a simple lunch of turkey, avocado, and soft Brie on Italian bread. Bottled water and some carrot sticks accompanied it, which was hopefully enough. Being in the classroom, she'd worked up an appetite.

*What a change.*

She glanced around the drab teachers' lounge. The room looked its age. Furniture with the upholstery cracked and a filthy microwave didn't make for an appealing environment.

Jasmine often lunched with clients, with vendors, or with friends, all at high-end places. This career move she contemplated required an adjustment. Perhaps that was what she needed…a more humbling environment. A place where she could make a real difference. Contribute something meaningful to a child's life. The pretentious fashion world had lost its luster.

"Good morning!"

The cheery voice caught Jasmine's attention. She wasn't certain it was meant for her.

"Good morning." Jasmine smiled.

The woman touched Jasmine gently on the arm. She was of mature age, wearing a crisp linen pantsuit. Her strawberry-blonde hair framed her face, giving her youthfulness despite her years.

"I'm Dana Summers. The kids call me Miss Summers. You can call me whatever you want; I don't mind."

"I'm Jasmine Landers. I'm substitute teaching in room twenty-six."

"Oh, Mrs. Cage's class. She fell off a chair and broke her wrist."

"They told me at personnel the assignment could last a couple of weeks."

"Where else have you subbed before?"

"I haven't." Jasmine lowered her gaze.

Dana's expression turned serious. "You haven't?"

"No, I've never taught before. This is my first assignment."

"And they sent you *here*?"

*What does she mean by "here"?*

"I've never been to this part of town before. I was thinking I would end up at Rose Cliffs or somewhere near me."

Dana chuckled. "Oh, heck no, not if it's your first time. Those plum assignments go to all the favorites. You know how personnel can be…I'm room sixteen, so I'm right below you. Easy to find."

"Oh, thank you."

"What made you decide to sub?"

Jasmine put her sandwich down. "I needed to do something fulfilling. I had great teachers growing up, and I wanted to give back."

"Are you single?"

"Excuse me?"

Dana laughed. "I'm sorry, there I go sticking my nose where it don't belong. But now that you found a new job, all you need is to find you a man. Unless you have one, of course, but I don't see any ring."

Jasmine's jaw dropped, stunned by the bluntness of this woman.

"That's the last thing I need right now." Jasmine kept her tone even.

Dana sighed. "I've been waiting for my Prince Charming for years." She gazed into the distance, her expression wistful. "Well, if you need anything, let me know." Dana smiled and grabbed something from the fridge.

"One thing…where can I find the ladies' room?"

"Finding an adult bathroom in a school can be like pulling teeth. Fortunately there is one right outside here and another one above it on the second floor." Dana waved her hand toward a door.

"Thanks."

"But…the adult restrooms are usually locked so the kids don't get in there. Come on outside with me."

In the hallway, Dana walked over to a door and tried it. Locked. She pulled out a key and opened it for Jasmine.

"You'll want to get your own key from the office. Don't bother Miss B. She'll make you feel like you're asking her to go out and wash your car for you."

"Who's Miss B?"

"The receptionist. She's usually there when the subs arrive."

Jasmine's expression soured. "We've met."

"Oh, so you got a taste of Miss B. I can tell by the look on your face," the woman said, almost in a whisper. "Miss Bradford. Everyone calls her Miss B. That's short for b-i-t-c-h." Her voice dropped to barely audible. "Wait another fifteen minutes or so and Miss Johnson should be back from lunch. She's nicer. She'll give you a key."

Jasmine smiled. "Thank you for all your help. You've been very kind."

"Bless your heart. After a taste of Miss B, I figured you could use a little kindness." Dana disappeared down the hallway. Clearly, she ate her lunch elsewhere.

After a quick twenty minutes, Jasmine returned to the classroom.

"How much that cost?" Jamal was eyeing her suit.

"Good question, Jamal. That relates to our composition topic for today."

"Writing after lunch!" Lazarus screeched.

"We always do writing *before* lunch," Terrance said.

"Yes, well, I had other things on my mind this morning, like getting to know all of you. I felt that took priority over a composition." Jasmine grabbed a stack of notebook paper.

"How long Mizz Cage gonna be out anyway?" Dennis asked.

"I don't know." Jasmine maintained her focus. "Now follow along with me as I read today's writing prompt out loud…"

They argued with her. They challenged her. They stalled. They hemmed and hawed. But eventually, they came around to doing what they were supposed to do.

Jasmine became aware of a bell ringing in the distance but didn't connect it with her class. None of them were moving. In fact, none of them were looking at her, but several of the boys were glancing at one another.

"Don't you try to play her that way! Get going!" A woman stood in the doorway, screaming at Jasmine's boys.

They all groaned, got out of their seats, and filed out.

"They *hate* going to enrichment," the woman explained. "But they gotta go. My class left a few minutes ago for music. Your class goes to art."

"Do I go with them?" Jasmine grabbed her handbag.

"Where *you* teach before?"

"I haven't," Jasmine answered.

"This is your break," she said.

"I've had my lunch."

The woman rolled her eyes. "This is your planning period. Time set aside to grade papers, prepare for tomorrow, or do what everyone else does on their break—nothing."

Jasmine nodded.

"You only get forty-five minutes. Make the most of it." The woman walked into the classroom opposite Jasmine's.

She peered across the hall. A dry-erase board covering what was probably the old chalkboard. Curious. She glanced up. The sign "Tompkins" stood above the door.

"I'm Miss Landers. You must be Miss Tompkins." Jasmine approached the doorway.

"That's *Mrs.* Tompkins," the woman sharply corrected her.

*Did I just insult her by insinuating she's single?*

"Mrs. Tompkins," Jasmine repeated. "I just wanted to introduce myself since I'm subbing for Miss or Mrs. Cage."

Mrs. Tompkins produced a small, flat smile. "She's Mrs. Cage. You got the repeaters."

16

"The repeaters?"

Mrs. Tompkins raised a brow. "They didn't tell you? Cage's class is all kids who are repeating the fourth grade. All their friends have gone off to the intermediary building for grades five and six, so they hate being here. Good luck."

A smile snaked across Mrs. Tompkins's face, one that could almost be interpreted as a satisfied.

Jasmine retreated to the hallway to begin her break.

*My break.*

Forty-five minutes with nothing to do but think about that man. Why now? She'd forgotten if he'd mentioned he was from this area or not. Either way, the thought never occurred to her that she'd see him again. They weren't supposed to meet again. It was called a one-night stand for a reason.

But her body shivered from head to toe at the memories of that one night. Her core burned, reminiscent of the passion in that hotel room last December. She reached for her purse, and her hand quivered.

Could she be mistaken? A man who merely resembled him?

*No. It's him.*

A man with that kind of sexual prowess could not be forgotten. His deep voice. Solid build. Charming manner.

*Very insatiable in the sack.*

The dampness between her legs erased any lingering doubt.

If she wanted to take her mind off of him, she had to keep busy. This would be a good time to familiarize herself with the school. She gave herself a walking tour. Downstairs, she passed room sixteen. Dana smiled at her and waved, all the while lecturing to her class.

Jasmine discovered the library and filled her time familiarizing herself with the school's bookshelves. The boys weren't being challenged. They were bored with the mechanics of school and had no motivation. A more challenging work would make them think and ask questions. She found a copy of *Tender Is the Night*.

Later, back in room twenty-six, Jasmine asked the class if someone could name the author.

"F. Scott Fizwhoever," Tyrone answered.

"Fitzgerald," Demetrius corrected him.

The boys had come back from enrichment in a much better mood. For a group that allegedly hated enrichment, it sure livened them up.

The afternoon came to a close without a lot of hassle, although they were so wound up it was hard to get a word in with them.

"Miss Landers," a voice crooned over the intercom.

"Yes?"

"Dr. Davis would like to see you on your way out today."

"Yes, ma'am," Jasmine said. Her body chilled and her skin turned to gooseflesh. Nervousness surged through her at the anticipation of seeing him. Surely he didn't—

"You goin' to the principal's office," LeRoy said, his voice laced with menace.

Jasmine didn't assign them any homework and ended class with a lively discussion of cars since they liked to gab so much. They were testing her, but she didn't mind. She was going to get through this somehow. It was the only way she could be sure if she was choosing the right career move.

Stopping in the office, Jasmine was relieved to see Miss B was not on her perch. Another woman was seated at a desk farther back in the office.

"Are you Miss Landers?" the woman asked.

"Yes."

"I'm Miss Johnson, the secretary. I'm the one who paged you. You can go on in..." She gestured with a warm smile toward an open door.

"Miss Landers," he said with his powerful tone, rising to his feet. "Please have a seat."

*Why did he call me here?*

Jasmine chose a seat facing him. The nameplate on his desk read Dr. Monte Davis.

*Monte! That's his name.*

He was a tall man, at least six foot two. He wore a crisp shirt and sharp tie but had removed the jacket he'd worn earlier that morning. Moisture pooled between her legs. It was him no question. The man who had fucked her all night long in a hotel room last year.

*Monte.*

Returning to his seat, he placed his large hands on the desk in front of him and looked at her directly.

"Now, Miss Landers, tell me...just what are you doing here?

# CHAPTER TWO

The striking young woman appeared stunned by his question. He hadn't remembered her name, Jasmine, until she'd introduced herself this morning. But he'd never forgotten her. One of the most beautiful women he'd ever met, and the only woman he'd been with in the two years since his wife's passing. And it was just for one night in New Orleans last year.

His cock surged at the sight of her. Now, with her in his office, he'd best remain seated. His boner pressed against his pants.

A full head of long, shiny chestnut-colored hair framed her face, and her eyes were big. Brown yet outlined in hazel. And that suit…the well-tailored suit that hugged every curve on her body. She hadn't any lines in her face. He'd checked out her Facebook page earlier in the day, and it revealed she was of Cajun/Creole/Scottish heritage. Perhaps that's what produced such striking facial features.

"I'm substitute teaching," Jasmine finally said.

She was either going to play dumb or play hardball.

He took a deep breath. "Jasmine Landers. Successful designer of women's handbags, profiled in *Designer Daily*, products featured on *Good Morning America*, very impressive sales figures, and"— Monte squinted at his computer screen —"named Designer of the Year last year by the Southeast Association of Women's Accessories."

Monte looked up from his computer and sat back in his chair. Jasmine's creamy-peach complexion turned pink. Her breasts swelled against the fabric of her suit.

"What does that have to do with substitute teaching?" Jasmine shifted in her chair.

"You tell me."

"My former career has nothing to do with my ability to do a job."

"Former career? You haven't given it up."

"No, I haven't, but I am making a career move."

Monte studied her carefully.

*She dresses like a fashion designer.*

He glanced outside his office door. Miss Johnson sat at her desk, and he was certain she listened. He lowered his voice.

"Why?" he asked.

"That's not relevant to the work I'm doing here," Jasmine said coolly.

"I'm not saying it is. I'm asking you why you're here. I don't recall any other high-end designers substitute teaching." He grinned.

He hadn't remembered any details about her except that she was exceptionally striking. He couldn't recall her career until he checked out her profile, and it hadn't surprised him to discover she designed handbags.

"I'm here because I'm contemplating a career move. I want to do something worthwhile, to feel as though I'm making a contribution. Mr. Whitney suggested I sub in a long-term spot rather than day to day. So here I am."

Monte frowned. Calvin Whitney interviewed all the substitute teachers in the personnel department.

*So he steered her here.*

She looked like she'd just stepped out of a pressure cooker. Her gorgeous hair covered her ears, but Monte was certain they must be red.

"I didn't mean to put you on the spot, Miss Landers. It's just common sense to research a new hire, that's all."

Jasmine glared at him.

He couldn't determine if her expression signaled discomfort or anger.

"Your BFA is from Florida State." Monte gazed at her bright red lips.

"You've done your homework."

Monte admired not only her beauty but her strong-headed nature as well. She certainly had a forceful personality that set her apart from substitute teachers who had come before her.

But he hadn't fucked any of them. He'd fucked Jasmine, though. All night long. And now, he wanted to do it again.

Monte rose and closed the door. "New Orleans."

She looked away.

"So you do remember?" His face went warm.

"Of course." She nodded. "I thought you'd forgotten."

"Never." His heart pounded in his chest. "When I saw you—"

"You didn't say anything."

"I didn't think it appropriate to bring up in the classroom first thing in the morning. But I couldn't wait any longer. I had to let you know that I remembered." His hands were sweaty, but he didn't dare wipe them on his pants. He didn't want her to know the effect she had on him. Not yet, anyway. Not until he got what he wanted. If anything.

"Why bring it up at all?" Jasmine asked.

"Dr. Davis," crackled the old desktop intercom.

"Yes?"

"Sorry for the interruption, but you're needed in the cafeteria. Flo won't let the after-school kids eat their snacks again," Miss Johnson said.

The problem with managing employees was that they were too set in their ways. Flo probably didn't even like children.

"I'm sorry to cut this short. We have an after-school program here, and the cafeteria manager throws a fit if the kids actually *eat* in the cafeteria. She has a phobia of crumbs."

Monte got up and gently brushed against Jasmine's shoulder on the way out. A bolt of excitement ran through his arm. This was dangerous. Monte couldn't recall the last time a woman had caused a surge to run through his body from casual contact. Actually, he could recall. It was *her*, nearly a year ago.

That one night in New Orleans. A night of drinking followed by casual sex in a hotel room that lasted all night long until the sun came up.

*That I remember.*

"See you tomorrow, Miss Landers."

Monte walked down the hallway, headed toward the cafeteria, but his mind was on Jasmine. She could model her own handbags she was so good-looking. His blood pressure spiked at the sight of her. When she had walked into his office, his heart had palpitated making him react more like a teenage boy than a man. He needed to clear his head and focus on the business at hand.

He adjusted his cock, which tented in his underwear, into a more comfortable position.

*How can I work in the same building as her?*

Alluring. Sensual. A reminder of a night that shouldn't have happened.

*She's a substitute. She won't be here long.*

It had to be coincidence she landed at this school. A successful fashion designer wanting to leave that career and become a schoolteacher? It was certainly admirable. It took a special person to do that.

Monte had followed a traditional path. He received his bachelor's in education when he was twenty-two, master's at twenty-five, and doctorate at thirty-two. He'd never leave the profession. And Jasmine's initial foray into the field was right under his roof.

*What really brought her here?*

After dealing with the trifling drama in the cafeteria,

24

Monte returned to his office. A quick glance outside revealed there was still about an hour of daylight left. He grabbed his jacket and slung it over his shoulder.

Outside his office, his secretary tapped on her keyboard.

"See you tomorrow, Miss Johnson."

"What do you have planned for the rest of the day?" The older woman didn't look up from her keyboard.

"A visit to the cemetery."

Now, Miss Johnson looked up. "Grief is necessary, but it's time to move on."

"Have a good day, Miss Johnson." He ignored her last words. She meant well and had almost become a motherly figure in some ways. But she didn't know that what he and Ellie had could never be replaced. But if the still-hard cock in his pants indicated anything, a little sex wouldn't hurt as a distraction.

The cool air did nothing to squelch the fire in him. Jasmine had sat across from him in his office, played it cool, and it had taken all of his might to resist her. The heat in his groin. The tightness in his chest. Memories of the time they'd spent that December night.

The last person he expected to see walk onto his campus, and yet she had. This morning. A stunning figure who came from out of his past. He was thrilled that she had, but uncertain what move to make next.

Monte steered his vehicle across town to the cemetery. After he parked, he strolled through several lanes of graves until he came to the resting place of his wife. He stood and stared down at the ground, still consumed by unbearable loneliness. Two years and the struggle continued. Everything reminded him of her. His house, which was the home they'd shared. Sleeping in the same bed at night, now alone.

Every time he visited her grave, he waited for the tears to come. They never did. He took a few deep breaths, trying to lift the heaviness in his heart. He tightened his fists. He couldn't cry and move on. Yet he continued to visit and stand over her burial plot, hoping for some closure. He prayed for strength, and each time he left, he didn't have the answer.

Each day after work, he returned to his house, the silence inside every bit as difficult to bear as the day she'd died. He clenched his fists and stared at the engraving on her stone. Hard to believe it had been two years. During that time, except for one night in a New Orleans hotel, he'd been so alone. So painfully alone.

Now, the alluring woman had walked into his life again. But for what purpose? Mere coincidence or fate? One way or another, he'd find out. The teacher who'd been injured was scheduled to be out for at least a week. And her substitute, the pretty young lady he'd met last year, had stepped into his life again.

*Jasmine.*

# CHAPTER THREE

As Jasmine jammed her key into the ignition, she wasn't sure which bothered her more—that man checking out her Facebook page or his graze against her shoulder that made all her tension melt away. And her cheeks burn.

*How can one touch do that?*

That simple gesture on his way out of the office sent a wave of heat through her. She'd experienced that touch with him, among other things. He probably made love to women he'd met in bars all the time. She couldn't make the mistake of being alone with him again.

She hadn't given much attention to men since a bad breakup a couple of years ago. Everything else in life had seemed to go well. A thriving business. Income larger than ever. And then, her relationship with a man who betrayed her.

On the surface, it had all seemed great with Chad. Romantic dinners. Occasional weekend getaways. Decent sex. But then, she'd found out he'd lived a double life. Another woman in a nearby town. A child she never knew about. It had all come crashing down when the woman showed up looking for him. An ugly end to something that had been fulfilling.

Now, Jasmine wasn't about to give Monte any attention. He gave *her* a good deal of it, though, or was it merely in her imagination? He hadn't called her into his office to discuss fashion design.

And how could that one night come back and haunt her? Counting the number of times she'd thought of him would be impossible. So perfect. So daring. So satisfying. Just what a one-night stand should be. A good one, anyway. Unfortunately, he'd ruined her. How could any other man compare to his stamina? She hadn't done anything so adventurous since. In that one night, he'd done so much. Stimulated spots she hadn't even known she had.

*So what the heck? How did I end up at his school?*

Jasmine had vaguely remembered he worked in education. Or at least she'd assumed. There'd been some kind of education conference going on at that hotel the same time as the fashion expo.

This had to be a coincidence. He'd been so drunk that night in New Orleans that he couldn't possibly have remembered her name.

*New Orleans.*

What a night. Funny how, eleven months later, she'd run into him again. Monte. How many times had she called his name that night? She shook her head and chuckled.

A man with his skills never had to be alone in bed. Unless he wanted to be. He probably had pickup lines saved in his phone.

As she maneuvered her Lexus across town, she pondered his subtle cologne.

*Goodness gracious, how did that creep into my head?*

She didn't have an answer, but she wanted to get close enough to inhale and let her sense of smell do the rest.

*I have to put him out of my mind. I can't be thinking about a man who is, for all intents and purposes, my boss.*

Jasmine had been toying with the idea of going back to school to get her master's degree in education. After ten years in the fashion business, she wanted a change. Fashion had begun to feel superficial. Her friend Louise suggested she should substitute teach and determine if she liked it.

When she had decided to explore a new career, she hadn't expected to walk into a school and find Monte as her principal. Sure, she was a sub and could leave at any time. But she'd made a commitment to the personnel department, and she had every intention of honoring it.

Jasmine turned onto the main expressway, heading away from Old Portsmith and toward her end of town. From what Portsmith once was in the eastern part of town to the modern hub in the western part of town. She had come across quite a few characters in that school, and some of their ways seemed old-fashioned.

*Cedar? Sandalwood? Perhaps a hint of cinnamon? What is the scent of that cologne he's wearing?*

When Jasmine arrived home, she kicked off her shoes and placed her suit aside with her garments that needed dry cleaning. She leaned against the kitchen counter. This was one of her favorite rooms in the house. The décor was inspired, at least partially, by her aunt's kitchen. Jasmine and her aunt shared a love for tchotchkes. The four ceramic jars in bright red lined up side by side, filled with cookies, coffee, tea bags, and sugar. It was a good room to unwind in, especially after a long day at work.

First day on the job as a substitute teacher, and the principal turned out to be the last man she'd slept with.

*Wow.*

That one December night came back to haunt her today. A night of letting go. A selfish night of sex, unlike any other night she'd experienced. Moisture pooled between her legs.

*How can I go back to Brookhaven tomorrow?*

So many depended on her now. Those eleven boys. Mr. Whitney, from the human resources department. She couldn't bail on them after only one day.

*But how do I face him?*

And that bullshit in his office. It would make sense for a principal to research a new hire, but she wasn't an employee. Just a sub to fill in until the regular teacher returned.

In the bathroom, she prepared the hot water for her bath. She needed one after today. A nice hot bubble bath with candles and music. The day had been fraught with tension after seeing Monte again, and Jasmine craved the soothing heat of a nice soak in the tub.

Steam rose from the water, and Jasmine tested it with her hand. Satisfied, she stepped into the frothy pool, leaned back, and closed her eyes.

*That night.*

Climax after climax. Monte's strong body above hers,

pleasuring every part of her. His mouth roved everywhere, his tongue probed deep, and his big, thick dick hit spots. Again and again.

She'd never come so hard and so often with any other man but Monte. Would it be so horrible to have a repeat session?

After Jasmine woke, she lay in bed on her back, staring at the ceiling. Birds chirped outside her window, the start of a new day. That night, so long ago, seared into her memory and her dreams. Today, she'd have to face him again.

As she prepared to return to Brookhaven, she rummaged through her closet. She'd obviously overdressed the day before, so she chose something understated. A simple skirt and blouse would do for today. And sensible shoes.

Her lingerie drawer beckoned. Not that she had the most extensive collection, but being a designer herself, she had access to an array of styles. The drawer slid open and Jasmine gazed inside.

As much as it pained her, she searched for something to wear for him. Not that he'd ever see it. But she'd know she wore it, and that was enough.

*It's also insane. Why am I thinking about that man now?*

She pulled a pair of black lace undies from Caroline's Boutique. Perfect to wear under her black skirt. Her hand glided along the silken fabric. What had gotten into her? She hadn't opened this drawer in…forever.

The smooth lingerie slid up her legs and covered her sex. Barely. Like something else she'd like to cover her sex—

Monte's mouth. As it had that night. Sucking on her clit, he'd brought her to orgasm after orgasm.

*This is gonna be one helluva day.*

It wasn't long before she pulled her Lexus into a guest parking spot at Brookhaven. Stepping into the office at school, she was greeted by an unfriendly face—Miss B.

"You came back?" she asked incredulously.

Jasmine avoided any conversation with her and signed her name and arrival time into the logbook.

"Wallace! Twenty-six!" Miss B shouted into her radio as Jasmine headed out the door.

Jasmine placed a foot on the step to go upstairs, then she paused. She turned around and walked down the hallway to room sixteen. Dana was seated at her desk, shuffling some paperwork. Jasmine knocked on the open door.

"Good morning!" Dana chirped, looking up.

"Good morning. May I come in for a moment?"

"Sure, come in. I was just fixin' to grade some papers. Pull up a chair. How did it go for you yesterday?"

"It went fine."

"Well, you came back. Some subs don't, you know." Dana rolled her eyes.

"Dana," Jasmine said cautiously, "what happened to Mrs. Cage?"

"Well, I told you yesterday, she fell off a chair and broke her wrist."

"In the classroom?"

"Yeah," Dana answered. "Why?"

"Any chance she was pushed?"

Dana looked at her bug-eyed. "Of course not! Where in the world did you get an idea like that?"

"I don't know." Jasmine shook her head. "It was just a thought that popped into my head."

"Good grief! No," Dana said. "Mrs. Cage is a union rep. She would have raised a ruckus, and I mean it would have been all over the television. What made you think such a thing?"

"All those viral videos you see on the 'net these days."

Dana waved her hand. "Don't pay any attention to those. There's always two sides to every story, and the media's only gonna show you the sensational part."

"Have a good day, Dana."

"You, too."

As Jasmine ascended the stairs to the second floor, suddenly consumed by images of Monte. The school day hadn't even begun yet, and he was already on her mind.

Jasmine found twenty-six unlocked. The classroom appeared how she had left it, with the addition of a cleaning. The floor had been swept and the trash emptied. Jasmine took a seat behind the desk and stared at the empty classroom.

Teaching would be a more structured life. Her day would begin and end at a set time. No working well into the early-morning hours on new designs. Perhaps she would find balance in her life, something that had so far eluded her. Balance between working hard, which she always did, and having a social life.

*Or having a man.*

Jasmine sighed. She could have had plenty but wasn't

interested. So why now, as she was trying to focus on a new career move, was Monte on her mind? He'd be a distraction. Exploring the teaching profession and getting aroused every time she caught a glimpse of him was not a good combo. She made a mental note to buy a bottle of shampoo on the way home.

*Maybe I can wash him out of my hair.*

A portly, older man appeared in her doorway, and he appeared to be studying her, if his roving gaze was any indication.

"Can I help you?" Jasmine asked.

"I'm Mr. Albertson, the assistant principal. We didn't have a chance to meet yesterday."

His expression hard, Jasmine didn't feel at all welcomed by him. Nor did she welcome his gaze roaming up and down her body.

"Usually our subs are old retired teachers. We're not used to having someone so pretty."

Jasmine turned her attention away from him.

"I've seen a lot of subs come and go. I've extended some of them outstanding recommendations and their careers flourished. Others, not so much."

Jasmine gripped the edge of the chair and resisted the urge to laugh at the absurdity of his chauvinistic way of thinking.

"It pays to be nice to your superiors," Albertson said.

"I'll keep that in mind," Jasmine answered without looking at him. She regretted the snarky tone as soon as she spoke.

Albertson's face turned red and his posture stiffened. "Sarcasm your second day on the job doesn't get you off to a good start."

Jasmine opened her mouth to apologize, but he'd already moved out of her doorway and line of vision.

*Great. An adversary.*

# CHAPTER FOUR

Monte arrived at work later than usual, having stopped to pick up a shrimp po' boy. Although he'd tried not to let his mind wander, it did. To Jasmine. The night they'd met had been one of the most sexually charged nights ever. Her creamy legs parted for him the whole night. Her lips had hungered for him, and she had the distinction of being one of the few women who could keep up with him.

If even just for that one night.

How much he wanted to relive that night again. Make it anew. Sustain it over time. Keep going. Would Jasmine be receptive?

Miss Johnson handed him a few slips of paper.

"Anything urgent?"

"No, just the usual. The art teacher wanted to see you for a minute. You also got a call from Lafayette."

*So Lafayette is interested.*

Monte's chest tightened and his face went warm. A surge of excitement raced through him. A fresh start in a new town on the other side of the state. Lafayette might quell the loss that consumed him.

That could be the answer to everything. If he got the job in Lafayette, he could put his grief behind him. Sell the house filled with memories of Ellie. Finally escape the pain of losing his wife.

Monte clutched his fist and took a few deep breaths.

*I'll return that call.*

After a quick trip to the art room, he returned to the main office and glanced at the sign-in log for substitutes and gazed at Jasmine's name. He'd wished he'd remembered her name from that night last year. Questioned what would have happened had they kept in touch.

It hadn't happened that way because he hadn't been ready to move on. That night was a fluke. Out of town, the ambiance of the bar, the desire to release some tension. He shook his head and returned to his office.

He stared at the slip of paper with the name and number. He had a good career here, but it was wise to keep his options open. If he could get a job a step up from principal, it would be a strong, motivating factor in resigning from this district. But that would mean leaving so much. A school he loved. His nephew, who depended on him. Give up his home.

"Sir?"

He glanced up at Miss Bradford standing in his doorway. "Yes?"

"I'd like to go on home. I have a headache."

"Okay. Feel better."

Maybe an elementary-school office wasn't the place for her if a headache was an issue. He had sympathy for his staff, but Miss B often looked for reasons to leave early. Heck, the day had barely started.

Monte seldom went near the teachers' lounge. It served as a private oasis for the teachers to gripe and groan about the goings-on at Brookhaven. But today, he wanted to bump into Jasmine. See her again. Speak with her. But not in front of any other staff members.

If he caught her after she'd dismissed her kids for lunch that might be the best option. No, as she only had twenty minutes, that would intrude on her time. Perhaps on her break when the kids went to enrichment.

A glance at the clock confirmed he still had hours to go before he could see her. It'd be difficult to function with the constant reminder of the night they'd shared. He had become stiff between his legs.

Finally, when her children were dismissed to their enrichment class, he made his move. He glanced into her doorway. Jasmine sat at her desk checking her phone. She wore a lovely white blouse and a slender black skirt.

Her tits jutted out in front of her. The blouse caressed all of her curves. Her creamy white legs, crossed, looked good enough to part.

"Miss Landers, excuse me for interrupting you."

She glanced up from her phone. "What can I do for you, Dr. Davis?"

He took a step into the room. "You can start by calling me Monte."

Jasmine turned her attention back to her phone. "Why? I thought staff in public education were formal."

Monte took a deep breath. His heart pounded in his chest. So much he wanted to say to her, yet this wasn't to place to say it. "There's a restaurant called the Blooming Cactus on Greenapple Road. Do you know it?"

"Yes." Her tone was flat and noncommittal.

Long chestnut hair fell far past her shoulders and her eyes were wide and bright.

"Please join me after school. There's something I'd like to discuss with you."

"Good. There's something I'd like to discuss with you, too."

His heart raced. "Oh?"

"Albertson. He makes me uncomfortable."

She avoided his gaze. Was she interested or not? She'd come back today. She didn't have to do that.

"I want to speak with you about something else. But not here."

"I don't follow you."

"Jasmine—Miss Landers, there's a lot more I have to say. I want you to know what was going on with me at the time we met."

She shook her head. "I don't see how it's pertinent."

*Damn, don't push me away.*

"If you're here, under this roof, even for a short while, I want you to understand. Please, join me. It's going to be awkward for both of us, at least for me, if we continue to work here together without talking about it."

Silence for a moment. Then, she met his gaze and responded. "Okay."

"I'll see you when you get there." Monte looked for some reaction, but she'd turned away. He left her to finish up whatever she had to do.

He hoped she hadn't become aware that his voice had notched up an octave or two, as it sometimes did when he got nervous. Right then and there, he had wanted to tell her he'd regretted not getting her contact info back in New Orleans. But he couldn't. Not at school. Not in her classroom. That wouldn't be right.

Blood pumped through his dick. She could stimulate a man, and she made him feel like a champion in bed. The unbridled passion, the hours and hours of lovemaking. Heat rushed to his face.

Hopefully, she'd show. He couldn't imagine what she must think of him, making a fool of himself like that. He couldn't risk her not showing. It would be awkward sitting in a restaurant waiting for someone who wasn't coming.

Finishing his work for the day proved difficult. Images of Jasmine clouded his thinking.

*Damn, after all this time.*

She had slipped out of that hotel room and out of his life. Could this be his chance to reclaim what they'd had that night?

# CHAPTER FIVE

When the door to her room closed, she exhaled. Jasmine's face flushed with heat. Now, she had to discuss it. He was right about one thing—if they continued to work here together, they couldn't avoid it.

Jasmine let the file she held drop to the counter. For nearly a year, her dreams had been invaded by that encounter. That night had been something out of a fantasy. One of those things you dreamed would happen but never did. They hadn't just had sex. Monte had made love to her, over and over again, throughout the night.

Her heart rate increased, and she gripped the edge of the desk. Light-headedness came over her and she reached for her handbag.

She couldn't see him. Not now. Her focus was on re-inventing herself. Pursuing a new career. And, finally, pursuing her years-long dream of going back to college and earning a master's degree. The last thing she needed was a fling to tangle things up.

After she finished preparing for tomorrow, she grabbed

her phone and texted Louise. *Meet me at Nicolodi's.*

Jasmine needed to talk to someone about this, and it sure wasn't Monte. But she had said okay. She couldn't just leave him hanging. No, she agreed they had to talk about it. She hadn't agreed the conversation had to be now at the Blooming Cactus.

Her phone chirped with a text from Louise. *Was than an order? LOL.*

Jasmine sighed. She must have come across as desperate. Which was correct. Her ring tone went off. It was Louise calling.

"Hey," Jasmine said.

"What's up?"

"Remember New Orleans?"

"Last year?"

"Yeah. The guy I told you about?"

"What about him?"

"I work for him."

"What the…" Louise's voice trailed off.

"I told you I got a substitute teaching gig, right? Well, he's the principal."

"No way."

"Yes."

Louise chuckled. "Now what?"

"He wants me to meet him. I can't do that. Let's go to Nicolodi's instead."

"Jasmine, you need to talk about it with him. Not me."

"I can't."

"So you're gonna show up for work every day pretending

you didn't have the best sex of your life with your boss?"

Jasmine loosened her grip on the phone. Louise was right. "I hear you."

"Go meet him. Then catch up with me later and let me know how it goes."

Jasmine stood in the empty classroom. When she hesitated about something, it tore her up. She sat at her desk and tried to sort out her options. Go to him. Or run in the opposite direction. See him tomorrow either way.

Her fingers fiddled with a pen on her desk. She clicked it on and off, on and off, much like the students did.

*Monte.*

How could he come back into her life now? The timing sucked. She had so much to focus on now, changes to make. She couldn't allow herself to be seduced by him again, as she had that cold December night.

She slung her handbag over her shoulder and descended the steps to the first floor. After signing out, Jasmine left the school with a knot in her stomach. She wanted a new career, so she had to be here to absorb and learn as much as she could about public education. And if Monte proved to be a distraction, it wouldn't work.

A brief meeting. Listen to what he had to say, and go home. No drinks. Just talk. She turned the key in the ignition and was on her way.

Greenapple Road ran along the edge of Portsmith, parallel to the freeway. Jasmine found a parking spot in the rear of the restaurant but sat in her car after she'd cut the engine. Her body trembled, and she wanted to leave. But facing another day at school with baggage between them wouldn't be pleasant. Better to resolve it now and move on.

The afternoon sun, now lower in the sky, still provided some warmth. Jasmine approached the front of the restaurant, each step heavier than the last. And she stopped before the front entrance. She couldn't go inside and be casual with Monte and relive something that had happened in their past. Part of her wanted to put it behind her, but she hesitated. And when she hesitated about something, she erred on the side of caution. And fled.

*Coward.*

Multicolored lights surrounded the door, painted a dull cactus green. When she entered, she spotted Monte standing by the bar area. He was close to the window, and the direct sunlight on his shimmering complexion revealed a hint of copper.

When Monte spotted her, he smiled and gestured for her to join him. Tall and with a brazen air about him. The tie gone, his shirt open at the collar, and that twinkle evident in his eyes.

"Thank you." He stood.

"For what?" Jasmine asked.

"Joining me."

The server placed two drinks on the table. "Can I get you anything else?"

"Some extra napkins, Wendell," Monte said.

After Wendell retreated, Monte turned to Jasmine. "The salsa can be messy." He took a sip of his drink.

Jasmine stared at the aquamarine concoction in front of her.

*So much for no drinks.*

"How did you know?"

"Blue Moon Martini? Facebook is a dangerous thing." Monte smirked.

He looked cute when smug. If he'd Googled her to find out her background, it was no surprise he'd trolled her Facebook profile.

"I want you to know I appreciate your successful work." Monte raised his glass.

"What made it successful?" The times Monte had shown up in her classroom, the kids weren't there.

"The students like you. They respect you. I think you inspire them."

"You haven't observed me in the classroom."

"I don't have to. I can pick up on it from the demeanor of the children."

Jasmine nodded. They weren't here to discuss Brookhaven Elementary but, rather, a night of nonstop sex.

Monte had taken the lead that night and never let up. She'd surrendered to him, completely, in a way she'd never surrendered before. And it was so damned good.

If there was one quality she admired most in a man, it was confidence. In the case of Monte, there was plenty more than merely sexual confidence. His large hand engulfed his drink glass and his eyes drew her in. They glimmered and captivated Jasmine in a way that made her not yet completely comfortable with him.

"It was an awkward couple of days."

Monte nodded. "I know. It was your first time teaching. It had to be."

*He's not making this easy.*

"Monte, we're not here to talk about school." Her stomach, hollow with nerves, rumbled as she reached for a tortilla chip.

"But you said you wanted to talk about Albertson."

"That can wait. I brought that up before you mentioned—"

"Will you be needing menus?" Wendell set some extra napkins down.

Jasmine shook her head. "I'm not hungry."

"If you want anything, just say the word," Monte said.

Wendell disappeared.

Monte leaned forward. "What has Albertson done?"

"Typical male bullshit. Pulled rank, even though I could care less because I'm only a sub. Made an awkward comment about being nice to superiors. Dangled the carrot of a recommendation."

"He's done that before."

"Then why does he still work there?"

"It's complicated. Public education is seldom simple. And now that you're entering the profession, what will you do with your business?"

"Are you really interested in all that?"

"Yes. We didn't discuss it in New Orleans."

*He finally brought it up.*

Just the name of that city conjured up images of passion.

"No, we didn't." But they had enjoyed one another's company, at least in the physical sense. Tongues meshed all night. Pounding after pounding, one climax after another.

"How did you get into design?"

*Why does he keep going back to that?*

"I focused on my passion."

"Tell me about your passion." Monte raised his glass.

*Is he kidding? He unleashed it for a whole night.*

Jasmine held his gaze before answering. "At the time, it was designs for women. I found something I loved doing and built a successful business out of it. Like many things, though, with growth often comes change."

"Go on."

*And why is he so interested?*

"I worked hard. I took a great deal of pride in my work. Others took notice. I still enjoy designing. I just don't like the business end of it so much. It has its own set of personalities."

Davis let out a hearty chuckle. "I can understand that only too well. If you don't mind my saying so, you come across as a woman who can handle her own with anyone."

*What's that supposed to mean?*

"How so?"

"You're strong. You've demonstrated that at school with the way you handle the kids and interact with the staff."

Jasmine took another sip of her Blue Moon. The gin and curacao blended perfectly together.

His Givenchy stretched across his full, muscular pecs. The white undershirt beneath the Givenchy blocked any peek at his chest. That barrel chest she'd dug her nails into when she'd ridden him in New Orleans.

Jasmine looked away. The last thing she wanted was for him to notice her staring at his pecs.

"Monte, you're young to have earned a doctorate."

"I'll be thirty-eight this month. It took a good six years or more of hard work. I was very determined."

"You should be proud of your accomplishments."

"I am."

*His birthday's this month. Scorpio? No wonder he's so good in bed.*

"What do you do with your time on the weekends?"

"I have investments. Some are profitable and some are not. I tend to those to keep busy. Eventually, I will let go of some of them. I just like being busy at the moment. Yourself?" His voice was smooth as silk. Barry White had nothing on Monte.

"Visit with friends and my aunt. Read. Travel on weekend getaways. Tend to my business interests as well, when I have to. I don't make a habit it of it."

"What *do* you make a habit of, Jasmine?" His playful gaze held hers.

*Where is he going with this?*

"How is everything? Can I get you another round?" Wendell perched by the edge of the table.

"No, thank you," Jasmine said.

"We're fine, Wendell."

After the young man left, Jasmine asked, "Is Wendell host, server, and bartender?"

"No, Wendell's my nephew," Monte said.

"Oh." Jasmine raised her Blue Moon martini. "Here's to family."

But she wasn't thinking of family. Rather, of Monte.

How cool he played it. All business. Was that what he intended when he'd wanted to meet her outside of school? Somehow, she found him sexier when he talked business.

"Here's to us—" Monte said.

"There's no us, Monte." Jasmine placed her glass down.

"You didn't let me finish. I meant to say us reuniting again after so long." He took another sip of his drink. "I'd like—"

"A repeat of New Orleans?" Saying the name of the city made Jasmine's heat level rise. So many memories of being ravaged in his bed, throughout the night. How many times had she wished for that night to happen again?

"A good time is worth repeating."

Jasmine dropped her gaze. Warmth spread across her cheeks and moisture pooled between her legs. "That's what I was thinking. They way you've looked at me. The glances I've stolen at you." Her heart raced. She was treading on dangerous terrain.

"It was a night I couldn't forget." Monte spoke in a low tone.

She leaned forward in a futile effort to inhale his cologne. *Can it work?*

"For what purpose, Monte?"

"Would you believe me if I told you I like what we had?"

"I believe you." She wanted another roll in the hay. What did he want?

"Are you that opposed to it?"

She hoped she hadn't come across as insensitive. It wasn't her intention to wound him. But there was that old expression that crept into her head. Something about not repeating a one-night stand.

"Of course I'm not opposed. That's why I'm here. I wanted to listen to what you had to say."

*And undress you with my eyes.*

Her heart about to burst out of her chest, she took another swig of her Blue Moon.

"I appreciate that." Monte took a deep breath. "I haven't been with anyone else."

Jasmine let out an involuntary giggle. "I'm sorry."

"You find that hard to believe."

"Yes. I'm sorry, I shouldn't have laughed. But that was eleven months ago, Monte." A man like him? If he picked up one woman in a hotel bar, he could do it anytime he wanted. He had the right pickup lines. Smooth as silk.

"It's the truth," Monte said.

"Would you believe me if I told you neither had I?"

*Why am I admitting that to him?*

"Yes," Monte said, his tone serious.

Jasmine gripped her napkin and twisted it. She might have hurt his feelings. Of course she'd assumed he was a stud, bedding random women for one-night stands. But perhaps she'd been wrong. The drink had given her a bit of a buzz. With or without alcohol, she wanted him again. She'd done little but think about it since they'd met again.

*No need to be modest.*

His smile had captivated her when they'd first met. How he'd focused exclusively on her, even though the hotel bar had been full of people. She'd left New Orleans with memories to last.

She'd missed his touch. More than that, she did want to get to know him. She'd have to give it some deeper consideration. Maybe this was a good time. When she wasn't subbing at the school any longer, there'd be no conflict of interest. But what could come out of it? Some endless nights of passion? Or deep disappointment?

"What attracted you to the profession?"

*He's all business tonight.*

"I've been yearning for a career change. The fashion industry is no longer for me. I love the work, and I love to design. But it isn't fun anymore. Dealing with the sharks in the business took its toll."

*Sure, keep this line of convo going.*

"I'm not familiar with the industry."

"It attracts a great deal of pretention. People who think they're bigger than the work they're doing. Egos the size of Canada."

"Got one or two of those in public education."

*Like Albertson.*

"In fashion, it's the norm." Jasmine clutched the hem of her skirt. "Besides, I had a major blow. One of my former assistants started producing knock-offs of my designs." Jasmine lowered her gaze. "It got ugly."

"That must have been difficult."

"It still is. I continue to do what I do out of contractual obligations. But my heart and soul aren't really in it anymore." Jasmine glanced out the window. Almost a year ago that the betrayal happened, it still seemed like yesterday.

"Foster on line one," her assistant had said, one breezy day last March. Foster was one of her distributors. Jasmine had taken the call and listened carefully.

"You're kidding." She'd known full well Foster did nothing of the kind. She'd quickly looked up the website Foster dictated.

"Wow." Her heart had sunk, and she'd exhaled in disbelief. Her brow had broken out with sweat, and her fingers, resting on the keyboard, had gone numb. There they were…knock-offs of her designs. Jasmine had listened as Foster explained who was responsible for them. It was one of Jasmine's former assistants.

Lawsuits had followed and Jasmine had known it was time to move on to something more rewarding.

"What drew you to teaching?" Monte paused. "Jasmine?"

She snapped out of her reverie. "I was guided to it. I'd been searching around for some type of volunteer work to do. Online, I came across a posting for a tutor. I thought, 'Hey, I can help some kid with his homework after school.' It turned out to be one of the most worthwhile things I've ever done. I got so much out of it. I'm sure I learned as much from him as he learned from me."

"That's awesome. I love hearing stories like that. The tutoring part, I mean."

Jasmine smiled. It was refreshing to be able to sit and have a professional discussion with him. At least they connected on more than one level.

Although what did he really want? Why did he take such

an interest in steering the convo toward education?

Finding a job without his help wouldn't be a problem. Public education craved new teachers, if Brookhaven was an indicator.

After another thirty minutes or so of cloying conversation, Jasmine grabbed her handbag. "It's time I get going."

"I'll walk you to your car."

She nodded.

They stepped outside into the cool air. The temperature had dropped since earlier in the day.

"Not my favorite time of the year." Jasmine peered at the dark sky.

"You miss the long days of summer?"

"Yes."

The rear parking lot was even darker and oddly secluded. Jasmine wouldn't have been safe coming back here alone. She clutched her coat close to her body.

"I enjoyed your company," Monte said once they'd reached her car.

He had that look in his eye, the one Jasmine had come to recognize so easily in the past two days.

"Thanks for the drink." She touched his arm, and her fingers landed on his bicep.

*He's solid as a chunk of chocolate.*

"We can talk about it now."

"Monte." Jasmine shook her head. "I'm not sure…"

*Talking can lead to more.*

"But I am, Jasmine. I need to tell you how good that night was for me."

"You were drunk."

"Not drunk. Just had a good buzz on. Had I been drunk, I wouldn't remember as much as I do."

"Such as?"

As soon as the words came out of her mouth, Jasmine regretted them. She'd just invited him to talk about it. That night. The desire. Sex until dawn.

"Every detail of your beautiful body. The way your warmth felt pressed against mine. The pleasure of being inside you."

Jasmine squeezed his arm, whether voluntary or involuntary she wasn't sure.

He placed his hands on her hips, pulled her to him, and his full lips met hers. Heat raced through her. Monte pulled at her lips with his and held her even tighter. One of his large hands slid up her. With her body still quaking, his tongue pushed through her lips.

Jasmine threw one arm over his shoulder, clutching him. His tongue sent a rush of warmth through her belly, warmth that she hadn't known with anyone else. She'd waited a year for this, never knowing if she'd have him again. The years of being so career-focused that she'd made no time for men, followed by that one night of unbridled passion with Monte. And now, tonight, she had the chance to reclaim that passion.

Her core ached with a want and need she hadn't known before she'd met him. When she tasted him again, she wanted him. All of him. She'd become so wet inside she was sure she'd need a change of her Guia La Bruna underwear.

*This is crazy.*

A low, groaning sound came from deep within her throat. She pulled away from his mouth, looked up at his dark brown eyes, and gasped for air. Her purse had dropped from her shoulder. Monte picked it up, and Jasmine quickly fumbled for her key. She turned away from him and jammed the key into the door.

"Monte, I'd better go."

He held the door for her as she situated herself behind the wheel, her breath still not regulated.

"Have a good night. Don't be shy about reaching out to me if you'd like to talk." He stepped back and pulled a business card from his pocket. "This has my mobile number on it, when you're ready."

Jasmine took the card from his hand but avoided his gaze. She nodded and turned the key in the ignition.

He closed the door for her.

As she backed out of her parking space, she glanced at him as he stood and stared at her. How could they get to know one another when all she could think about was that night? Of course she wanted that again. What woman wouldn't want a man who made love until the sun came up?

But he'd made an overture to her. Could she "get to know" him? Or had she gotten to know all the parts she needed from him?

At thirty-two, men hadn't been a large part of her life. It was all about the career. With no parents or siblings, it had fueled her focus. To become driven. To succeed. And for what?

To reach a point where she was willing to give it all up and teach. And what happened while exploring that career for the first time? Walked smack into Monte. A man she'd craved more times than she'd like to admit. A man whose touch she'd dreamed about at night.

She had the weekend to forget about him. Focus on her career shift. Get those college applications filled out and look forward to some campus visits next week. At least for the local colleges. She still had her eye on one out-of-state school.

But what if she couldn't handle the work? She'd been out of college for a decade and times had changed. Courses were probably all online now. Did anyone even show up for classes anymore?

Those were questions she could research this weekend.

*If I can take my mind off Monte.*

# CHAPTER SIX

"Who was that?"

Monte spun around, startled that he wasn't standing in the parking lot alone. His nephew stood in the darkness, barely visible in his black host's uniform.

"What are you doing out here?" Monte asked.

Wendell shrugged. "I'm on break."

"On break in the back parking lot?"

His nephew had spied on him. Probably followed them out of the restaurant. Wendell didn't have any other male role models in his life and could be possessive of Monte. Although Wendell had friends his own age, he spent a good deal of time pursuing things to do with his uncle.

Monte's heart went out to him. Monte's own childhood wasn't as lonely. He'd lost his family much later in life, when he was at an age mature enough to handle it. Wendell's world had shattered early on.

"So, who was that?"

"You've seen me here with co-workers before."

"Not that one."

"She came to Brookhaven this week."

Wendell shifted his weight from one foot to the other and looked at his uncle with those doe eyes. One would think, by age nineteen, he'd grow out of being so clingy. But he had a vulnerable side that came out all too often.

"She drives a nice car," Wendell said.

"Yes, she does."

A hardworking, self-made woman. Jasmine had an inner strength he admired. She'd followed her passion, not a traditional path, and had built a successful career.

"What's her name?"

"Why do you ask?"

"I heard you call her Jasmine."

"So you know her name."

His wife had wanted the same thing, in a way. She'd had a passion for home décor. Yet a fierce commitment to her job—she'd worked tireless hours as a teacher long after the dismissal bell had rung—had prevented her from seriously pursuing anything artistic.

Jasmine, in a sense, straddled the best of both worlds. She'd done what she'd wanted to do with her creative side, and now it was time to pursue something more meaningful. He wanted to nurture her, but Jasmine would neither need nor welcome it. Far too independent, she blazed her own trails without any help.

"I thought in education you addressed teachers by their last names. They call you Dr. Davis, and you call her Miss—"

"Landers. You're right. My mistake." It wasn't lost on Monte that Wendell had been fishing for Jasmine's first and last name. But why?

"Where are you going now?"

"Home," Monte said. "Now get back to work."

"So is she the one?"

"The one *what*?"

"You're not gonna be single forever."

"Wendell, get back to work before your ass gets fired."

His nephew turned and headed back to the Blooming Cactus. Monte watched him go inside and then returned to his car.

*Poor Wendell.*

The boy was too emotional for his own good. Wendell's reactions were sometimes melodramatic. He'd had a rough childhood. Shipped around from one foster home to the next, until Monte finally reconnected with him. Monte's sister, no longer living, had abandoned him long, long ago in a town far away. It was sad and tragic, and it had taken years for Monte to find him. Now, Wendell attended college, had a job, and had a bright future if he could stay focused on priorities.

Jasmine had appeared conflicted, and that was understandable. After one long night in a hotel room out of town, they'd never expected to meet again. But what they'd shared couldn't be denied. There was a connection there, a powerful one. He wanted to explore it and hoped she would come around.

*Without the pressure of being near each other all day.*

The pressure in his pants was another issue. He wanted to recreate that night, and do it often. He admired her tenacity. To abandon a successful career as a fashion designer in favor of teaching was admirable.

And yet he couldn't have her. Not in that way. The memories of his late wife lingered. He cherished those memories, held onto them, and took comfort in them. He couldn't let go of that. Being with another woman would diminish the happiness he had with his wife. He couldn't allow himself to feel anything for her. It had only been about sex.

Ellie had been the love of his life. After her death, he hadn't overcome that loss. It had been foolish to think a night of sex could quell that pain.

What he and Jasmine had had in New Orleans was a fluke. It wasn't supposed to happen. Nothing planned, just opportunity and one martini too many. Now, he couldn't look at another woman. Jasmine had come into his life at a time when he'd needed her, even if for just one night. Nothing would come of it.

*Lie again, Monte.*

He'd denied himself long enough. Sex couldn't be the only thing that came out of seeing Jasmine again. Reuniting with her after so long was worth more than that.

He didn't plan on letting her get away this time.

**

Louise's house wasn't far from Greenapple Road. When Jasmine arrived, Louise stood in the kitchen experimenting with a new Creole dish.

"So how'd it go?" Louise wiped her hands on a kitchen towel.

"Okay, I think."

"You think?"

"I'm not sure what he wants from me."

Louise shook her head. "You'll see him tomorrow."

"I know, but I don't feel comfortable."

"Tell him that."

Jasmine nodded.

"Sit down. Taste this and tell me what you think." Louise placed a small bowl and a spoon on the table. "If it works, I might bring to for the dinner after services on Wednesday. Are you going?"

Jasmine shrugged. She scooped up some of the concoction with a spoon and savored the flavor. A blending of bold spices, the shrimp etouffe made other recipes pale in comparison.

"This is awesome," Jasmine said.

"Thanks. Now, what are your options?" Louise asked. She twirled the ringlets of her hair with one finger. Louise, an aspiring chef, spent a good deal of her free time whipping up new dishes.

Jasmine placed her spoon down. "I can get reassigned."

"Jasmine, this is your first time working as a substitute teacher. Ever. What reason will you give them?"

Jasmine shook her head. "I don't know."

"How are the kids?"

"Great. They're the reason I'm there."

"Then you should stay there."

"It's awkward."

"So what options do you have left?"

"Avoid him. Or jump into bed with him."

She couldn't continue avoiding him. Not only would she see him at work, she'd be constantly reminded of what pleasure she'd experienced when they'd first met. She wasn't accustomed to a man having that effect on her.

"Do you think you could have done it?" Jasmine asked.

"What?"

"Balance a successful career and a relationship."

Louise sighed. "I'm not sure. When I was married, being a wife was a job and a half. At least with the man I chose as a husband. Now that I'm back in Louisiana and toying with the idea of starting a business—I'm still not sure. I certainly wouldn't turn a fine man away just because I had career goals."

Jasmine nodded.

"But you can do it." Louise met her gaze.

"Why do you say that?"

"You're established in your career. Even if you're starting a new one, it is possible. You just have to make it work." Louise gestured to Jasmine's bowl. "Eat the rest of your etouffe before it gets cold."

Jasmine dug her spoon into the succulent dish and enjoyed every bite. She'd worry about tomorrow...tomorrow.

"I've said this before, and I'll say it again. You should open up your own restaurant. Or catering business."

"Yeah, I think about it a lot. One of these days I'll do something about it."

"Louise, you know I'm looking into going back to school. I wasn't planning on a man."

"The good ones are *never* planned."

# CHAPTER SEVEN

The next morning, Jasmine parked her Lexus in front of Brookhaven and stepped onto the asphalt.

Dana Summers struggled to remove some bags from the back of her Honda.

"Let me help you," Jasmine offered.

Dana's face lit up. "Oh, you're so sweet. I raided the dollar store last night…just grab a couple, and that'll be fine. I always overspend when I go to that place. You know, it's called the dollar store for a reason. They want you to think you're gonna walk in the door and spend just a dollar."

Dana breezed past the office.

"Shouldn't we sign in?"

"Sure, hon, after we put these bags down. Don't want Ol' Miss B snoopin' in my business." Dana smiled.

Down the hall, she unlocked room sixteen with her key, and they carried the bags in.

"Oh, just throw them on my table. Thank you. I appreciate your help."

"No problem."

"How's the class going?"

"I like it," Jasmine said. "The boys are a handful, but I'm enjoying getting to know them."

"Speaking of boys, what do you think about that dreamboat principal?"

"I don't have an opinion of him."

"He hasn't been the same since he lost his wife," Dana told her.

"Lost his wife? How so?" Jasmine asked.

"Oops, there I go shootin' off my mouth again when it's none of my business. I've said too much already. Um, shouldn't we go sign in?"

After they'd signed in, Jasmine ascended the stairway to her classroom still curious about when Monte had lost his wife. Before last December or since? Not that it mattered.

When Jasmine reached her classroom the door was unlocked. The trash bins had been emptied and the blinds closed. When she glanced at the chalkboard, she decided to start off the day with a bell ringer posted. Now, she needed to come up with an activity. She placed her handbag on her chair and inhaled sharply when she caught Monte standing in the doorway.

His scalp, shaved smooth, caught the reflection of the overhead light. The broadness of his shoulders could barely be contained in the doorframe. Even when he was dressed in a suit, it was apparent he exercised regularly.

She gazed at him, and her lady parts became moist. Her nipples pebbled against her bra, and she hoped her face didn't betray her arousal.

"Good morning," he said.

"Good morning."

"All I want is for you to be comfortable here. Are you?"

"No."

"What can I do to make it better?" Monte had a gleam in his that Jasmine recognized. She'd seen it before in New Orleans.

"You can't stop being you. How can I look at you without remembering?" The ache between her legs signaled want. She'd relived that night in her mind so many times. They'd met only weeks after a horrible break up with her ex. Monte had been in the right place at the right time to wash away some of the lingering pain.

"I have the same problem," Monte said and took a step forward.

Jasmine's body quivered. If he took another step closer, she might smell his cologne. That strong, masculine fragrance he wore—whatever it was called. She'd fall prey to his magnetism.

"We don't need to talk about this anymore," Jasmine whispered.

"I do. You're working under my roof. It'd be too awkward to pretend."

"I'm not pretending anything," Jasmine said.

"I am. Pretending I'm not attracted to you. Pretending I don't want to repeat that night. Pretending I'm not fighting the urge to see you as often as I can."

Her temples pounded, in sync with the rhythm of her heart pounding in her chest. The ache between her legs needed relief.

Wasn't that the point of meeting to talk last night?

"We can't," she said, her voice hoarse.

"I know. Not right now." Monte held her gaze for a moment. "I'll let you get ready for class."

After Monte left the room, Jasmine clutched the edge of her desk. If that was the effect he had on her in a classroom, what would happen if they were alone somewhere private? She pulled her hair and closed her eyes for a moment.

*This, too, shall pass.*

The kids would be here soon. She had to pull it together for them. Shaking from being so close to Monte again, she had a lot of pulling together to do. Working here was a challenge. Being in a public place, like a restaurant, was one thing. Being in a classroom…

Later, the morning's lesson went well. The boys were in a good mood and were actively participating in a lesson about the solar system. Satisfied she was getting through to them, she forgot all about Monte.

Less than an hour into the morning, Miss Johnson appeared at the door.

"Miss Landers, you have a new student."

The boys collectively groaned.

"Her name is Catherine Adams. I think her mother calls her Cathy. She'll be up in a minute. Miss B's entering her info into the system."

"Thank you, Miss Johnson."

"Yeah, thanks for the warning!" shouted Lazarus.

Miss Johnson gave Lazarus a stern look.

"She's also a repeater. That's why they placed her in your

classroom and not one of the other fourth grade classes," Miss Johnson said.

"Great, another loser," Dennis mumbled.

"Dennis, be quiet." Miss Johnson nodded and left the room.

Jasmine approached Dennis.

"Do you think you're a loser, Dennis?"

"No, ma'am," Dennis answered.

"Good. I don't either. None of you are losers. Please don't make that assumption about someone you haven't met."

A few minutes later, Cathy Adams entered the classroom, looking like she would rather be getting a root canal than joining a class of all boys. With a defensive expression, her brown eyes darted left and right.

"Good morning." Jasmine smiled. "I'm Miss Landers. "

Jasmine didn't think the front or back row would be welcoming for a newcomer, so she directed Cathy to a desk in the middle of the room. Cathy appeared to be somewhat prepared, as a notebook or two and some pencils were tucked under her arm. She lumbered toward her seat, which Jasmine attributed to new-student nerves. Jasmine had been teaching less than a week, and here she was making her own assumptions.

*I just took the boys to task for making assumptions.*

"Cathy, we're talking about what we would need to take with us if we went on a journey to explore a planet. You're welcome to participate, but if you're more comfortable just listening, that's fine, too."

Cathy didn't respond. Jasmine gave her some space and continued with the lesson.

"Demetrius, pick a planet."

"Pluto. And yes, it is a planet. None of this eight planets stuff here."

"I never said there were only eight planets, Demetrius. And I never will."

"Good. I don't like seeing Pluto get dissed."

The boys kept eyeing Cathy, and they seemed distracted by the fact that she was a new person in the room and a female. Jasmine chose not to address it and just kept the flow of the lesson and discussion going.

Pierre, seated closest to Cathy, said, "Which planet would you go to?"

Cathy turned her head away from him.

Some might've called her behavior rude. She didn't participate, and it was unclear if she was even listening. First days could be awkward for anyone, so Jasmine let her be. Her own first day at Brookhaven had been awkward.

*With good reason.*

The morning proceeded uneventfully until about thirty minutes before lunch.

"I don't like this seat," Cathy said out of nowhere.

"Is there something wrong with it?" Jasmine asked.

"No. I just don't want to sit here."

"Where would you like to sit?"

"I'd like to sit on your face," Cathy stated with a snarl.

Some of the boys laughed, but it sounded like a nervous laugh.

*Great. The class troublemaker has arrived.*

"That option is not available to you, Cathy," Jasmine responded coolly.

"I'm going to get up," Cathy threatened.

"Stay where you are," Jasmine said.

"When you turn your back, I'm going to yell that one of them groped me," Cathy continued, pointing to her classmates.

Jasmine turned on her heel. Her face became red.

"Cathy, as a woman, I find it disturbing that you would use your gender to make a false accusation against a classmate. Those kinds of harmful statements discredit women who really have been abused," Jasmine explained.

"I don't care." Cathy got out of her seat.

"Sit down, Cathy." Jasmine tried to remain calm.

Cathy slowly moved toward her. "You're not even a real teacher."

Jasmine didn't like this at all. She hated confrontation. "Get back where you belong, Cathy."

"You never taught before in your life. That old lady in the office told my momma everything about you. Seems you might be out of your element, Miss."

"I am the adult in this room, and you are not. So as much as you may not like it here, the same rules that apply to everyone else apply to you," Jasmine told her.

"Fuck rules," Cathy said.

"You watch your language in this classroom."

"Fuck you!" Cathy shouted and, with a powerful right hand, slapped Jasmine across the face.

The boys bolted out of their chairs. Several of them were on Cathy at once. Corey threw his body in front of Jasmine and held his arms out like a human shield. Cathy was strong. She wrestled free of the boys and got to her feet. Terrance pulled his arm back and punched her squarely in the eye. She staggered back a bit, and several boys jumped her and held her to the ground.

Across the hall, Mrs. Tompkins shouted, "Tell 'em to get up to twenty-six."

Within seconds, Tompkins entered the room and looked directly at Jasmine.

"Landers, get on your cell phone and call 911 *now*. And don't tell anyone I told you to, or I'll deny I said it."

Tompkins immediately left the room and went back to her class.

Dazed, Jasmine reached for her purse and pulled out her cell phone, all the while being protected by Corey. She dialed 911.

"Jasmine Landers. Brookhaven Elementary School. I've been assaulted." Jasmine tried to regulate her breathing. "I think it's at Twenty-Four Hundred Clover Lane."

The phone was still up to her face when Dr. Davis, Assistant Principal Albertson, and Wallace appeared in the doorway.

After the three men broke up the chaos, Jasmine put her phone away.

Monte and Wallace led Cathy downstairs.

Jasmine's body shuddered. She'd seen videos of this kind of thing on YouTube but never expected it to happen to her.

Not a good thing for her boys to see. She'd made so much progress with them in such a short time, and now a fight had upset her applecart. Spoiled her milk. Got her bitch-slapped.

Albertson got right up in her face. "Who were you on the phone with?"

Jasmine didn't like his tone. "Nine-one-one."

"Who told you to call them?"

"No one," Jasmine lied.

"Well, I hope you're satisfied," he said, practically spitting the words at her.

Jasmine got a burning feeling in her ears.

"I was assaulted," Jasmine said.

"Which adult witnessed it?"

*I can't believe this.*

"Miss—Mrs. Tompkins," Jasmine said.

"I'll be speaking with Tompkins. I saw your boys attack that girl."

"They were protecting me!"

"You're the one who'll need protection," Albertson said.

"What's that supposed to mean?"

"Get downstairs. I'll take care of your class."

From an office downstairs, where Jasmine gave her report to the police, she glanced out the window as Catherine was led away in a squad car.

*What a mess.*

Jasmine didn't need something like this before her career even started. She had heard the stories of teachers being assaulted by a student, but it was one of those things she'd put out of her head when she'd decided to accept the assignment. Her first week as a sub, and she'd already filed a police report.

*What a hot mess.*

She hoped Mr. Whitney wouldn't hold it against her. He had been so kind to her in personnel. It was his suggestion that she try long-term subbing rather than day-to-day. He said that would give her a better feel for the profession. She'd agreed with the idea so much that she reclaimed it as her own.

"I fixed you some tea."

Jasmine looked up as Miss Johnson stood in the doorway with a steaming cup and a Lipton teabag draped over the side.

"Thank you, Miss Johnson," Jasmine said as Miss Johnson set it down next to her.

"You look okay. A little redness on one side of your face, but it'll pass." Miss Johnson smiled and started to leave the room.

"Oh, Miss Johnson, how long do I have to stay here?"

"Let me check with the police. They might need to see you again."

It seemed like an eternity had passed, Jasmine sitting in a room with nothing to do, but she was eventually released. She picked up her purse and slowly walked out of the room and into the office. Her legs went weak, and her butt hurt from sitting.

"Dr. Davis wants to see you. He has someone in there right now, though," Miss Johnson told her.

*Great.*

Jasmine stood by the office counter and waited. She was anxious to get back to her class. After all, they were the reason she found this assignment so fulfilling. Bless Corey. He really cared about her. Terrance, all of them had pulled together for her.

Someone whom Jasmine did not recognize emerged from Dr. Davis's office. When the stranger left, he gestured for her to come in.

"I'm sorry this happened to you. It's rare we have any kind of incident at Brookhaven. Since you pressed charges, the student will not be allowed to return to here."

"That man was so damned rude to me."

"Albertson? Ignore him. He has no power here."

"He acts like he owns the place."

Monte sighed. "I assure you he doesn't. He's been after my job for years. I can only imagine the stuff he says about me behind my back. We don't have a school nurse here. Can I have someone drive you to a quick care?"

"It's not necessary."

"Then will you go on your own, please? You should have that shiner checked out."

Jasmine let out a slight laugh. "I think I'm fine. There's one in my neighborhood. I might stop by after school today."

"Take the rest of the day off. You'll be paid for a full day."

"That's not necessary."

"To get paid?" Monte grinned.

"No, to take the rest of the day." The students needed a teacher.

"Please. I'll feel much better if you went to quick care. Now's as good a time as any."

"I'm not leaving my students." But she'd do about anything to leave his office. Being with him alone in a room made her body heat rise.

"Let me call the district nurse. She can come here and examine you."

Jasmine nodded. "Fine. I need to get back to class."

Monte nodded. "Thank you." He picked up the phone.

His concern for her warmed her insides. Concern, or was it a fear of liability?

# CHAPTER EIGHT

Her hips swayed from side to side as she stepped out of his office. She wore a classy skirt and a brightly laced blouse. His gaze stayed on her behind, and he recalled how his hands had held that ass in bed. It seemed so long ago.

Something stirred between his legs and he sat behind his desk. If this was the effect she had on him, something had to give. He couldn't be sporting wood every time he came near her. Not here, anyway. And he'd see her at school five days a week, numerous times throughout the day.

But he kidded himself. He hadn't been able to be with a woman since his wife. That one night with Jasmine was the first and only time. In the condition his heart was in, he had nothing to offer a woman. Memories of his wife consumed him and his dreams, happy memories that he wanted to continue.

*A woman would erase those memories.*

Monte gazed at the slip of paper on his desk with the message from Lafayette. A new job prospect in a new town. Immersed in work. No time for any distractions.

Maybe that was what he needed. But he had a job he loved and a nephew with no other family. Both needed him at the moment. Was that enough to stay? He'd always been ambitious. Always looked out for the next career move. Even if he didn't take advantage of the opportunities, he it was wise to scope them out.

"So, what are you going to do about her?" Albertson said after appearing unannounced in his doorway.

"About who?"

"That sub."

"I'm not going to do anything about Miss Landers, if that's who you're referring to."

"My suggestion is you call Whitney and have her replaced."

Monte held his gaze. "Miss Landers will remain here for as long as necessary. It's not your concern."

Albertson's face contorted into an ugly grimace before he disappeared from view.

The personalities in public education were challenging. The profession attracted too many of the wrong people. Like Albertson. Or that crazy cafeteria manager.

Jasmine's allure was dangerous. He wanted her again, no point in denying it. Those soft curves, her wet heat, the hours and hours of pleasure. Sure, he'd drunk a lot that night. Everyone had. What New Orleans bar didn't have a party atmosphere?

He remembered how she'd made him feel. Sated. A man. All man. Something special in her touch. Now, she'd inadvertently walked back into his life. Or had she? It wasn't supposed to be anything more than a one-night diversion.

When the phone rang, he'd lost track of the time.

"Davis," he said when he answered.

"Davis, what the hell's crawling up Albertson's butt now? He just called me going on and on about Miss Landers." Whitney sounded mad, but not nearly as pissed as Monte.

"He's being Albertson, causing trouble, and sticking his nose where it doesn't belong. Miss Landers is doing a fine job."

"I thought so. Later."

*Damn Albertson.*

Another six months of that pest before the school year ended. Monte had far more important tasks than dealing with that busybody.

*For instance, what do I do about Lafayette?*

**

When Jasmine entered Brookhaven the next morning, Albertson stood in the hallway by the office door with a smug expression.

"Since you pressed charges, Cathy will not be allowed to return to Brookhaven," Albertson said, practically spitting the words at her.

Jasmine was getting that burning feeling in her ears again. She turned her back on him to sign in.

*Oh, no, he isn't.*

"Why does your tone suggest I am being blamed for something?" Jasmine countered.

"Why don't you ask your boys? They've been dealt with."

"What do you mean by dealt with?" Jasmine demanded.

"They've all been disciplined. Terrance has been suspended. The others are going into the detention room until I determine their punishment," Albertson told her. "I've lightened your load, Miss Landers."

Jasmine's eyes blazed. "Those boys defended me!"

"One of them punched a student. Others put their hands on her. They've been disciplined according to district code." Albertson's smug grin tightened.

Miss B's expression revealed she enjoyed this a bit too much. Miss Johnson had the class to turn her back on the confrontation and busy herself at her computer.

"Albertson, get in here," Davis said, appearing in his office doorway. "Miss Landers, you can go on upstairs."

Her fists clenched, Jasmine bolted up the stairs to the second floor. Mrs. Tompkins was seated behind her desk. She did not look up when Jasmine appeared in the doorway.

"Thank you, Mrs. Tompkins, for your advice yesterday," Jasmine told her.

"I didn't speak to you yesterday," Tompkins said.

Jasmine stared at her for a minute. It was becoming clearer to her how things ran at Brookhaven. Jasmine turned around and walked into twenty-six.

*Wow.*

Public education was an adjustment. That would never happen in the corporate world, where people generally took responsibility for their actions. Folks in Portsmith seemed inured in the twenty-first century. They did thing their way, and they were not about to change.

How long could she go on ignoring Monte? What bothered Jasmine even more was another question: how long could she go on ignoring that warmth that permeated her every time she thought of him? She'd gotten that taste of him last year and wanted it again.

The heat in her core stirred and her eyes closed. When she recalled his touch, her whole body shivered. Her hand gripped the edge of her seat as she fought the ache between her legs.

"Miss Landers." There was a hint of cheer in Monte's voice.

Jasmine snapped her out of her reverie.

Monte stood in the doorway, as commanding a presence as ever. His slacks wrapped tightly around his tree-trunk-size thighs.

"I'm sorry you had to endure Albertson as soon as you walked in the door this morning."

"He was gloating."

"Yes, he probably was."

"Does he have the authority to discipline those boys?"

"Unfortunately, yes. That's his job."

"It isn't right."

"I wish it were my call. When I first arrived at Brookhaven, enrollment was small enough that it didn't warrant an assistant principal. As our numbers grew, we were assigned one. Discipline used to be part of my job, but now it's in his hands."

"It isn't fair."

"Many things in public ed aren't fair."

"I've noticed." Jasmine missed her boys already.

"On a different note, I wanted to give you a couple of names of people I know in higher ed." Monte stepped forward and handed Jasmine a folded piece of paper. "One is in elementary, the other in secondary. They should be able to answer a lot of your questions about an alt-cert program."

"Thank you." Jasmine took the piece of paper from his hand. Her hand brushed against his for a second, and heat rushed through her body.

"There are several colleges in the area that offer programs."

His gaze held hers.

"I've started researching some of them." Jasmine's heart thudded in her chest.

"I know you haven't been here long, but from what I've seen, I think you'll be successful."

"I appreciate you saying so." She inhaled and her breasts swelled. Why did he have to come to her room this morning? Couldn't he have just emailed her? Being in the room with him alone was not a good way to start the morning. Her lady parts were already aching.

"Have you decided on an area of study? Elementary or secondary?"

She recalled what it was like to have her ankles pressed against his broad shoulders. Not that she should be thinking about that now, but she couldn't help it.

"No. I've only been in a classroom a short time. It's too soon to decide."

Either it was hot in the classroom or her body heat had spiked considerably since he'd walked in.

"Understood. Have a good day, Miss Landers." Monte left the room.

Jasmine stood still for a moment and took a deep breath. She didn't want her students walking in and finding a red-faced teacher. She opened her bottled water and took a swig.

Aching with want, her pussy needed him. Long, hard, and deep. That's how Monte fucked, and she wanted him again. She was a fool to think otherwise.

But it was more than that. It had to be. No man could bring out this kind of a bodily reaction from her unless a deeper connected existed. It had to. In some way, that might be how she'd ended up here.

Could it be that Monte and she were meant to be? Or at least, meant to meet again and see how it went? Stranger things had happened in her life. Meeting him again could be fate.

For something more than just sex?

The boys arrived to class with higher energy than yesterday. Jasmine took that as a good sign. Pierre came into the room singing a rap song and announced he had written it himself.

"I respect your enthusiasm, Pierre, but this isn't the time to talk about your songwriting. I do encourage creativity. I would like to see you channel that into a writing assignment," Jasmine told him.

When time rolled around for lunch, Jasmine wasn't keen on the dreary teachers' lounge again. She wanted to be close to her boys and let them know she was there for them. So far, none of her students had mentioned yesterday's drama, and she preferred it that way.

"Hey, guys. Are you okay with me sitting with you at lunch?"

"Why?" Dennis asked.

"I'm sick and tired of the teachers' lounge already."

A few of the boys laughed.

"Join us!" Lazarus said.

The cafeteria was in sadder shape than the teachers' lounge. Old, creased, yellowed posters proclaiming *Drink Milk!* hung on the walls, pieces of old tape placed over more pieces of old tape to hold them together. Oddly, no menus were posted. Not even signs pretending the food had nutritional value. Rows of institutional-looking tables lined the room, some filled with students, others empty.

"Do you sit anywhere in particular?" Jasmine asked.

Jordan pointed to a table. Jasmine took a seat while the boys grabbed their meal cards and filed into the serving area. She gazed around the room. A tired-looking matron was propped up against a wall, presumably to monitor behavior or noise level. It wasn't working.

Jasmine waited until all her boys were seated before she started on her own frugal lunch. The tables sat ten comfortably. Jasmine sat with nine boys at one table, and the last two in the line were seated at the adjacent table.

Her boys, compared to the rest of the students in the cafeteria, were quietly eating their lunches.

"You two…move! I just cleaned that table!" shrieked The Wicked Witch of Brookhaven.

Jasmine looked up to see a grown woman with a hairnet pointing to the two boys at the adjacent table.

"They're fine where they are," Jasmine told her.

"Excuse me?"

Jasmine turned to the two boys at the adjacent table.

"Eat your lunch. You're fine."

"I'm getting Albertson," screeched the cafeteria worker.

Jasmine smiled and shook her head. This must be the cafeteria manager Monte had alluded to. The boys weren't smiling.

Albertson came bursting into the cafeteria and homed in on Tyrone and Demetrius.

"Get your butts out of those seats and move now! When Miss Taylor tells you to do something, you do it."

Tyrone and Demetrius jumped out of their seats. Taylor was ready with her finger pointed to another table, well removed from the rest of the class. Then Albertson turned to Jasmine, his face red.

"And as for you, missy, you're just a sub here, so stay in your own lane. We have procedures here. This is Miss Taylor's cafeteria."

Jasmine was stunned. She couldn't even respond to such petty nonsense. Albertson stared at her as though waiting for a response. She squarely stared right back at him until he walked away. Once he was gone, Jasmine picked up her lunch, tossed it into the trash, and ignored Miss Taylor's smug, self-satisfied grin as she headed out.

"Boys, don't go anywhere. I'll be right back," Jasmine told them.

Jasmine strode into the office, brushed past the staff, marched into Albertson's office, and slammed the door shut.

"I don't know where you were raised, and I don't care to know. It's bad enough the way you speak to eleven-year-old children, but I'm an adult. You will speak to me with respect or not at all. I don't care how you talk to everyone else here, and I don't care how they talk to you. I'm not putting up with it. You owe me an apology."

Albertson looked at her for a long time before speaking. "Are you recovering from a recent head injury?"

Jasmine ignored the snarky remark. "You lost it in front of my children. You can apologize to me in front of my children. I'll be in the cafeteria when you're ready."

Jasmine turned on her heel and was out the door. She pretended not to notice that Miss B's jaw had dropped and that Monte had poked his head out of his office.

Jasmine returned to the cafeteria. Most of the boys had already finished eating, which meant they must have wolfed it down. Jasmine sat calmly. She clasped her hands in front of her and waited. Some of the boys tried to speak to her, but she smiled and said, "Not now."

An indeterminate amount of time passed. After what seemed like eons, Albertson entered with Monte squarely behind his shoulder.

"Taylor, come out here for a minute," Monte said.

Taylor came out from the serving area. From the look on her face, it must have been a delicious canary.

"Miss Landers, I apologize for raising my voice with you." Albertson glanced at Taylor, and then back to Jasmine. "I could have handled that situation differently. Please continue doing the best work you can do with our children."

His face was red, probably from choking on his words. Or from the heavily starched shirt wringing his neck.

Albertson turned and left the room. Flo Taylor's face was in a knot, and she quickly retreated to the serving area without a word.

Monte winked at her and nodded and then left her alone with her boys.

*Monte must have ripped Albertson a new one.*

Jasmine couldn't believe how people spoke to one another in public education. In any other industry, they'd be sent home for such nonsense. In the short time she'd been here, Albertson's behavior seemed to be tolerated. She didn't understand how people could work with those kinds of unprofessional outbursts.

Jasmine finished off the day by showing the class a few scenes she edited together on her laptop from *Tender Is the Night*, a film adaptation of the F. Scott Fitzgerald novel. She watched the boys' faces as they watched the movie. They seemed to really be captivated by it.

After the film clips, she initiated a short discussion. Predictably, the boys had never heard of any actors in the 1961 film. They all agreed that the two female leads were two of the most beautiful women they had ever seen.

"That's because they were movie stars," Jasmine said.

"I like Nicole," DaShon said.

"That's Jennifer Jones," Jasmine responded, "and she was a beautiful woman."

"I'll take the other one!" Pierre exclaimed.

Jasmine smiled. "I object to your use of the word *take*,

but I see what you mean. Joan Fontaine lights up the screen."

At the end of class, LeRoy presented her with a handmade card.

"We made this for you in art class this week," LeRoy mumbled.

"Thank you, LeRoy," Jasmine said, looking him in the eyes.

Jasmine looked at the front of the card. It was a painting in watercolor, presumably of her, labeled "Miss Landres." They almost got the spelling right. Inside, "Thank you for all that you do for us. Please stay." It was signed by all eleven boys, and her eyes misted as she stared at it. Jasmine gave each one of them a hug.

*This is working.*

# CHAPTER NINE

Monte stared out the window grateful this day had ended. He'd never had an employee like Jasmine who stood up to Albertson. Or Taylor, for that matter. It was about time someone did. She brought strength and common sense to the job, two things that were sorely lacking in public education.

"Miss Landers is here to see you," Miss Johnson announced.

"Come in." Monte stood from his desk with a broad smile, although standing might not be such a good idea.

Jasmine stepped into his office. Her mane of chestnut hair fell beyond her shoulders, and her silk blouse shimmered in the afternoon light. Her breasts were visible in the low neckline.

"Please, sit down," Monte said.

"I won't be long."

"What can I do for you?" He reached for the door.

"Leave it open. I'm on my way out."

"Is there a problem?"

She clutched her handbag, slung from her shoulder, and

balanced her weight on one foot. Her hand rested on her hip. Fire seethed in her glare and her lips pursed.

"Yes. Albertson. That's the second time in two days he's bullied me. If that's the way ya'll treat one another here, then maybe I don't fit in with the adults."

*I can't believe she just said ya'll.*

"Those boys need you."

"Albertson doesn't, and I don't need him and his crap."

Monte frowned. "I know. He's been a problem here for a while."

"So why is he still here? In the corporate world, he'd be fired for that."

*Of course, she's right.*

"This isn't the corporate world and sometimes that's unfortunate. Mr. Albertson has a contract. He can't be terminated unless he does something really stupid or harmful. Please, stay for those boys."

"I'm not accustomed to being spoken to that way by anyone, and I'm not about to start now. If he does it one more time, I'm making a formal complaint. In writing. Unlike him, I don't have a contract, and I can walk anytime I want."

Monte nodded. "True. But I hope you won't. The kids like you."

*I like you.*

"I can't be an effective teacher if I'm being bullied. If you're not able to do anything about it, I'll speak with Mr. Whitney."

Monte's posture stiffened, along with his cock. "That

won't be necessary. I'll see what I can do with Albertson on my end."

*She's tough.*

"Wouldn't you have done it by now? I can't be the first one he's bullied."

"To be honest with you, Miss Landers, you're the first one who stood up to him. I admire that quality."

*And so much more.*

"I can't come to work every day and fight off lecherous assholes like Albertson."

"Forget about him."

"You told me public education attracts the wrong people. Something tells me he's not an exception."

Monte shook his head. "On this campus, he pretty much is the exception."

Jasmine raised a brow.

"Okay, him and Miss B."

*Formidable.*

"Still, it's not encouraging."

"Look, you told me the people are what turned you off to the fashion industry. Now you're saying the same thing about public education."

"So it's me?" She shifted her weight from one foot to the other.

"Jasmine, I'm not saying that at all. Look at what you've accomplished. You're leaving behind a very lucrative, high profile career for a business where you're going to make a low salary. And that salary won't go up much as long as you stay in the classroom. It takes a great deal of courage and commitment to do what you're doing."

"I don't really see it that way."

"You take risks. I believe people who become truly successful, or at least happy, are those who take risks."

"And you haven't?"

Monte shrugged. "Not really. I've been doing what I'm doing for fifteen years. Sure, I moved up. But I started teaching at twenty-two. I'm thirty-seven now, and still working in a school building. I don't see going from teacher to principal as all that much of a risk."

*Fifteen years.*

Played it safe. Stayed in the same industry. Jasmine had taken the opposite path. Took risks. Built her business from the ground up.

"Still, it's hard work."

"Jasmine, what you're doing is brave." Monte didn't want to say it, but she'd inspired him to grow. Change produced growth, and she grew as a person by taking risks. He'd done none of that. But now, he had to take the risk of letting go. Not in his career but in his personal life. He had to let go of the hold he had on his late wife. Or was it the hold she had on him? He hadn't grown since her death.

Yet her death signaled a major change in his life. He had to learn from it and explore his own growth. With Jasmine, he could do that. When he'd met her that night in New Orleans, he'd taken a major personal risk.

Picking up a beautiful woman in a bar might be nothing for other guys, but for him, it had been a big step. Then, nothing. No further growth.

"Please, tell me you'll stick it out."

"I'll do it for the boys. I owe it to them."

"No, Jasmine. You owe it to yourself. This is your future."

"That sounds..."

"Selfish? It's not. You have to think of yourself. You have to be happy and in a good space to teach these kids. They pick up on everything. They can read every mood. It fascinates me every day to deal with these kids and see just how observant they are."

Jasmine nodded. "You're right about that. I've noticed it, too."

"Thank you."

"For what?"

"Speaking to me about it. Allowing me to listen. I hope I've been of some help."

If he could help her, maybe he could reach her on another level. They'd had sex, but nothing else. He didn't want it to end with a one-night stand. He'd denied himself pleasure for so long.

"Yes. Maybe my career objective should be to become an online teacher. That's the way of the future, isn't it? Online instruction. Kids staying home."

Monte laughed. "I don't think it's the same thing. I doubt it will come to that. Public education is a very greedy industry. All of their money comes from attendance. The school districts aren't going to give that up, no matter how much it benefits the kids."

"So it's not about the kids?"

"Public ed in general? No. It's all greed. It's the greediest industry I've seen. Millions and millions of dollars are funneled into districts every year, but hardly anything improves. There are classes here that don't even have the required textbooks. I can call central, fight with them, argue some more. But I always get the same answer. They claim they have no money."

"And it's a lie."

"The biggest lie in public ed is to hear any official say they have no money. Especially a Title I school like this."

"Title I. That means?"

"Bank." Monte chuckled.

"I don't follow you."

"That was a bad attempt at humor. Title I means a majority of the kids on free or reduced lunch. The school gets a truckload of federal funding because of that."

"Right. I think you mentioned that before. Or someone did. I have a lot to learn.

"You will, Jasmine. Look around at some of the folks here. You're going to shine."

"Thank you for your help."

Monte closed the door behind her. That had to be the longest they'd spoken at school. He hoped she would follow through with her goal, for she'd certainly make a great teacher. The potential was all there.

He sat at his desk aware of the tingling in his groin. She had that effect on him. At Brookhaven, that already distracted him.

# CHAPTER TEN

A bright, sunny Friday morning, it was also the last day of the school week.

*Went by quickly.*

The boys had grown on her. She looked forward to seeing them. That's what education should be all about—the students. Not trolls like Albertson.

During her break, Calvin Whitney from personnel came to her classroom.

"Miss Landers, I'm sorry to take up your time on your break. I wanted to tell you personally that Mrs. Cage is returning to work on Monday. "

"Oh," Jasmine muttered.

*I'll miss my boys.*

"Dr. Davis has praised you like none other. I've never heard such kind words about a substitute teacher before. He spoke of your professionalism, your dedication to your students, and how much of an impact you have had on their lives in your short time here."

*Is he joking?*

"I have another assignment for you on Monday, if you would wish it. It's at Vista Terrace Middle School, and it's an eighth grade English Language Arts class. The teacher has known for a while she would be taking a short leave, so you will have all your materials and lessons prepared for you. I think you'll be ideal for the job," Whitney said.

Jasmine smiled. "I'll take it."

"That makes me happy. Based on what Davis has told me, we are very lucky to have you. He's a tough leader, and I've had many subs not last one day here."

*That I can believe!*

Whitney handed her a sheet of paper. "I've printed out the details for you. At the risk of sounding like I'm repeating myself, I've never heard Davis speak so highly of anyone before. You've certainly made a strong impression here."

*He's repeating himself.*

Jasmine reflected on what Mr. Whitney had said about her. If Monte had said those words to a third party, he probably meant them. He certainly didn't have to do that. Perhaps she had made a difference here.

Jasmine couldn't decide if she wanted to announce it was her last day or just quietly say goodbye to each boy as he left. She opted for the quiet goodbye and hugged each one of them as he left the room.

After the school day had ended, she remained in her classroom for some time, gathering up her things. She wanted to make sure she left the room in a neat condition for Mrs. Cage.

"Mr. Whitney told me the news."

Jasmine gazed at Monte. "You have a habit of showing up in my doorway."

*Looking gorgeous.*

"I'm sorry to see you go."

"It's for the best." Getting away from his allure. His charm. His masculine scent.

"Not for the boys."

"That doesn't indicate a high regard for Mrs. Cage."

"I didn't mean it that way." He didn't have his jacket on and his sleeves were rolled up, revealing his muscular forearms.

Jasmine turned away from him and placed some folders into a book bag. She didn't want him to see the effect he had on her. The flushed cheeks. The buzzing in her ears. Her heart palpitating against her chest.

"It won't be awkward anymore."

She glanced in his direction, but he was now closer. He'd taken several steps forward, and he stood only a foot or two away from her. She couldn't help but hold his gaze, her breathing deepened.

"I know," she said.

*But it's awkward now.*

"Monte." She said his name in a breathy voice.

Her hand rested on his hairy forearm. The one thing she didn't want to do yet desired so much. She had memories, too. His wet, passionate kisses. His robust body on top of hers. His massive dick pounding into her all night, making her come over and over again.

Monte slid his arm around her waist and pulled her close.

His lips tightened and his gaze penetrated her. The look in his eyes was one she'd seen before. Her cheeks flushed with heat.

*Resist.*

Jasmine inhaled his manly cologne and squeezed her grip on the hard muscles of his forearm. The heat of his breath scorched her face. Her lips parted, and he pressed his lips against hers.

She became light-headed, as though the room spun. His kiss. That warm, wet kiss she'd savored so many times in one night. His touch could do that to her. A night of passion that had done so much more, and she wanted that again.

The core of her womanhood burned with want. Every fiber of her body yearned for him. If only she could surrender to him right now and feel that satisfaction again.

Monte's arm roamed along her body, sending pangs of pleasure throughout her. Fire raged in her, filling her with a need she hadn't had since that night in New Orleans.

He lifted her by her buttocks and placed her on the desk, and her legs parted. With one arm, he knocked almost everything off her desk. A folder full of papers splayed across the floor.

"Monte, this is crazy." Jasmine clutched his strong arms, and his muscles flexed under her fingers. She gripped him the same way she had in that hotel room last year. Moisture pooled between her legs. She wanted his cock in her again, thrusting and pounding like he'd done that night long past.

"I'm crazy. I never should have let you go that night. Never should have resisted you all this week. We should have picked up where we left off when we found one another." His voice breathy, he gazed into her eyes.

"We weren't looking for each other." Her chest tightened. She'd been reminded of him night after night and wished she'd remembered his name.

"No, but I thought of you. Often. Relived that night over and over again." His mouth close to hers, she wanted to dart her tongue out at him.

Jasmine nodded. "I've done the same."

Monte's tongue found hers, and she hungered for it. He tasted of peppermint candy. She hooked her arms around his neck so he couldn't pull away.

"Jasmine." He said her name as though it were a revelation. His arms tightened their grip on her. "I haven't stopped thinking about you this week."

"We're on a desk."

"I know."

"In a classroom."

"There's no one else here," Monte whispered into her ear. "We're both working late tonight."

Jasmine glanced at the window. It was already dark outside. She'd lost track of the time. They were on the second floor. Although the school was in a remote part of the neighborhood, surely someone could spot them.

Dampness welled between her thighs and she parted them farther, longing for relief. She wanted him—right here, right now. The ache. The need. They all added up to one thing.

"Please," she whispered, wanting so badly to get fucked right here and now.

Clanging metal.

Monte broke away from her.

"You heard that?" Jasmine asked.

Monte nodded. "The night custodian. I'd forgotten all about him."

Jasmine slid off the desk and smoothed her clothing. She grabbed her handbag and tote.

"Jasmine." Monte whispered her name.

"Not now, Monte. I have to go."

When she reached the bottom of the stairs, the night custodian had an industrial-sized bucket. He paused mopping the floor. "You okay, Miss?"

"Yes, James. Had some cleaning up to do in the classroom."

"Get home safe, Miss."

"Thank you."

Jasmine left the building and walked down the stairway to her car. The night air, now chilly, filled her lungs. The coolness relieved some of the fire burning within her. Monte would have taken her right then and there on the desk, and she would have let him. A year was a long time to go without a man. But she'd never seen anyone after Monte because no one could live up to his prowess.

She tossed her bags in the back seat and then glanced up at her classroom window on the second flood. Monte stood in the shadows of the room, gazing at her. A shiver ran though her, and she wished she were back in that room with him—on that desk.

The time had arrived to stop denying herself. Monte was right about one thing. Now that they didn't work under the same roof with temptation lurking around every corner, why suppress what they both wanted? They could reignite that flame they'd started in New Orleans.

As Jasmine drove home, she looked forward to a hot bubble bath with some soothing music. She'd survived one week as a substitute teacher and was optimistic about her career move.

*He wants me.*

No matter how much she tried to push Monte from her mind, it didn't work. Who was she fooling? She wanted to reclaim that night. Find out if it was a fluke, or if something deeper had happened. A connection.

*I can't ignore him.*

# CHAPTER ELEVEN

Saturday, Jasmine sat before her laptop in her home office. Many of the colleges and universities offered either fully or partially online programs. Not that it really mattered, as a degree program would require an enormous commitment of time.

A rush of exhilaration swept through her. Going back to college had been her dream for years. If it weren't for the responsibilities of running her fashion business, she would have done it a long time ago.

Louise had reminded Jasmine that she would find a lot of online degree programs she could earn from home. But regardless of whether she attended a local college, an out-of-state university, or an online program, pursuing a new relationship at the same time would be challenging.

*Can I not think about him for just one minute?*

Master's degrees in teaching elementary education, early childhood, special education, secondary math, secondary social studies, and the list went on and on. Overwhelmed by the degree options available, she needed to focus on whatever other details could factor into her decision, such as faculty, location, fees, course offerings, and so much more.

Excitement rushed through her when she considered the possibilities. The challenge of going back to school had her pumped and ready to roll. Despite a successful career, it had always been a dream of hers to return to school.

*College, here I come.*

"Is there anything else I can do for you, Miss Landers?"

Jasmine spun around. She'd been so engrossed in her research that she hadn't been aware Martha enter the room. Martha had kept Jasmine's house clean for the past four years, and Jasmine had gotten accustomed to the good work her housekeeper did. A gray-haired, stout woman, Martha was a single mother who'd had her one child when she was in her late thirties.

"No, thank you, Martha. I won't be needing anything else today."

"Are you expecting a guest? I could prepare something," Martha offered.

"No, I'm not. Why do you ask?"

Martha frowned. "The car that kept passing your house. I noticed it when I was cleaning the living room."

Jasmine's attention heightened. "What car?"

"Beat-up old blue car. Some rusted paint, a few dents."

Jasmine didn't know anyone who drove such a car. "What kind of car?"

Martha shook her head. "I don't know anything about cars. If my son were here, he would know."

"Did you see the driver?"

Martha shook her head again. "No, I didn't. Not that I didn't try. The windows were tinted."

Jasmine's lips tightened. The last thing in the world she needed was a stalker. She had no idea who would do something like that.

"Martha, would you prepare something? A tea service sounds like a good idea right now," Jasmine said quickly. She didn't want to be alone at the moment.

"Yes, ma'am."

"How are you getting home today?"

"My son is picking me up."

Relieved, Jasmine smiled. "Okay, don't do anything fancy. Just tea and light sandwiches will do."

That would give Jasmine a little time to decide what to do…if anything. That car could have been driving by anyone's house on this street, yet Jasmine trusted Martha's instincts. If Martha suspected that the car was driving by this house, then that was all Jasmine needed to hear.

"What time will your son be here?"

"I haven't called him yet."

"Take your time." Jasmine turned and tried to focus on her computer, but she found it hard to concentrate.

*Who keeps driving by?*

She shook her head. Nothing was going to be gained by stressing out over it. Jasmine had bigger fish to fry, like a master's degree. She focused on her research and lost track of the time.

"Anthony is here," Martha announced.

Jasmine almost jumped out of her skin.

"Sorry." Martha apologized after Jasmine jumped. "The tea service is ready. It's in the sitting room."

"Thank you, Martha."

"Can I get you anything else?"

"No, I'll be fine. Please tell Anthony I said hello. I didn't even hear his car pull in."

"It didn't. He sent me a text that said he's about a minute away."

Even Martha had entered the age of the text message. Her son had most likely gotten her started on it. Anthony had a good job at a hospital, and he made his mother proud. Jasmine had been so engrossed in her work that she forgot to invite someone over for tea.

"Invite Anthony in for tea," Jasmine said.

Martha was halfway out of the room when she turned. "Ma'am?"

"Sure, why not? You went through all the trouble of making a tea service. Let's enjoy it." Jasmine didn't want Martha to detect how unnerved she was about the mystery vehicle cruising by her house.

Anthony was an interesting young man, about twenty, with wild hair and funky clothing. Jasmine liked his style. Full of energy, all with a good sense of humor, something Jasmine could appreciate on this bizarre evening.

"What's up, Miss Landers?" Anthony had the most infectious smile.

"Hey, Anthony. Good to see you. Come on into the parlor and sit down."

"Thanks."

The sitting room, a small parlor off the vestibule, had a cozy ambiance. A couple of sofas, a few large easy chairs, and small tables with knickknacks filled the room. The color scheme was pale blue. She stole glances at the windows.

"Your mom made some sandwiches. Please, help yourself."

"Awesome." Anthony had a seat on the sofa.

"How's your new job going?"

"It's the best. Full benefits, good health plan. Paid days off! I never had that before."

Jasmine smiled. "It's about time. I know when I was your age, and younger, I worked an endless stream of part-time minimum-wage jobs."

"Yeah, that's history now. I like it at the hospital. Gonna stay there for a while."

Martha beamed as her son devoured her chicken salad sandwiches.

Personable and goal-driven, Anthony was also strikingly handsome with angular features and neatly maintained dreads. He'd be a good catch for a young woman.

Their presence provided a relaxing break, and Jasmine resumed work as soon as they left. Or, at least, tried to. Her heart still heavy, a strong sense of foreboding and solitude hit her as soon as Anthony and Martha were gone. The mystery car nagged at her, and she had trouble keeping her fingers steady on the keyboard. She wished Martha and her son had stayed longer.

On Sunday morning, Jasmine prepared to visit Aunt Harriet. She'd gotten up early and baked some sugar cookies. Weekly visits to her aunt were the norm since she'd moved back to Portsmith after college. Besides her aunt, she had no one. She clung to her childhood memories and relived them through her aunt, the only living link to her days as a young girl.

But something else had nagged her since she'd woken. Not just the creepiness of the car allegedly driving by last night but something more than that. The wife. Monte's deceased wife.

She marched over to her computer and started searching. It didn't take long to find.

*Eloise May (Glover) Davis, 34, died at Mercy Hospital on November 6th after a long illness. Born in Huntsville, AL, she was the daughter of Paul and Josephine Glover. She was educated in Louisiana, where she remained as a teacher. She had no children. In addition to her parents, she is survived by her husband, Monte Davis, her sister, Elizabeth Harper of Birmingham, and one niece, Sarah Harper. Visitation will be held Friday, 6-8 p.m., at Rogers Funeral Home. Services will be held Saturday, 10 a.m., at Morningside Baptist Church.*

So his wife had been a teacher. Jasmine couldn't recall anyone mentioning that before. Her death had occurred two years ago this month. Her mind raced. Had they met on the job? Was Monte retracing his steps? Had this been a pattern with him?

*I don't want to be a replacement for a dead woman.*

But she wasn't. Who could have done something as childish as drive by her house?

*Call it a hunch.*

Jasmine drove over to the Blooming Cactus and maneuvered her car into the rear parking lot, her eyes scanning for something. Her hunch proved correct. Sitting in the employee parking section was an old, beat-up, paint-deprived blue car.

"Wendell," Jasmine said as soon as she entered.

Wendell looked up from his post and quickly looked away.

"We need to talk."

"I'm working."

"Please, take a moment."

Jasmine led him to the outdoor eating area, which was empty at the moment. Jasmine wasn't certain of it, but she suspected Wendell was literally shaking.

"Look me in the eye," she told the nineteen-year-old.

Wendell turned his back to her.

"I'm not going anywhere."

Wendell rushed inside the restaurant. Jasmine hesitated. She had to remind herself he was only a teenager. She followed him inside. He darted around a corner, and she had a feeling where he was headed. After she waited a few minutes, Wendell emerged from the men's room.

"Tell me what's going on."

His gaze immediately darted away.

"Right here," Jasmine said, using two fingers to point to her eyes. Wendell tentatively met her glare.

"You've been stalking me, and I want to know why."

Wendell shifted his weight from one foot to the other, looked away, looked at her, looked away, seemingly unable to focus.

"My maid saw your car drive by my house. Now tell me what's going on."

Tears welled up in Wendell's eyes. Jasmine was surprised by his reaction to mentioning his uncle. What was going on with this young man? He walked away from her, back to his station by the door.

Thankfully, the restaurant was not crowded. She'd come during that dead time between lunch and happy hour. Jasmine approached him at the host station.

"Talk to me, Wendell," Jasmine said softly.

Wendell muttered through his tears. His face was flushed. "Uncle Monte is all I have."

Jasmine's heart sank. She, too, had only her Aunt Harriet left as family. Poor Wendell. They had something in common. He only had an uncle.

"You are not going to lose your uncle to me nor anyone else."

*What has Monte told him about me?*

Jasmine studied his face but could discern no reaction. "Wendell, driving by my house is not the way to get my attention. Have you spoken to your uncle about this?"

Wendell shook his head.

"I didn't think so," Jasmine said. She placed a hand on his shoulder. "Your uncle loves you, and you're an important part of his life. That's not going to change."

"You haven't told him about this?"

"No, I haven't. I wasn't sure until now." Jasmine released her hand from his shoulder. "But you will. It's the right thing to do."

"I'm sorry, Miss. It was a stupid thing to do."

Jasmine stepped back outside the restaurant with a heavy heart. How sad for Wendell that, at nineteen, he had no one except his uncle. And how ironic the parallel it drew between her and Wendell. She wasn't angry with him any more but, rather, sympathetic. At least Monte was there for him.

Autumn in Portsmith was a beautiful time of the year. She breathed in the late- afternoon air as the day transformed to dusk. The leaves on the trees had turned, and many of them were scattered over the parking lot as she climbed into her car and drove home.

Was Wendell that insecure? Jasmine was puzzled by the steps he'd taken to frighten her. Was there something else going on that she didn't know about? Nineteen-year-old young men were usually more preoccupied with friends than family.

This whole situation with Monte had become overwhelming. She hadn't been involved with a man for a couple of years. That man hadn't worked out because he'd told her she was obsessed with her career. Monte appeared to be encouraging her, which was reassuring, but being with a man was not on the current agenda. As Louise would say, when it happened, it happened.

*But just what is happening?*

She needed an evening out. With a quick text to Louise,

she'd made arrangements for a drink tonight. That would get her out of the house and give her eyes a break from the computer.

"He's jealous of you," Louise said pointedly.

"I know," Jasmine groaned and took another sip of her wine. They were seated at a lovely wine bar on Petronia Avenue in the hip, upscale part of town. It attracted new people with new money. Jasmine liked the place because it was classy. People didn't flock to it merely because it was trendy but rather because they enjoyed the ambiance and good wine selection.

"No, really. He sees you as a threat. He could be dangerous." Louise stared at her.

Jasmine shook her head. "I don't think Wendell is dangerous. I think he's just kind of sad." Like herself, Wendell had no one but a single relative. But Wendell was so much younger, still a teenager. The adjustment was difficult, and Jasmine sympathized with his possessive hold on Uncle Monte.

Jasmine frowned. She had let her guard down with Monte. She had let this man into her world and into her psyche like no man before him. Monte had it all…strength, success, good looks, beautiful, muscular physique, and he was an expert in the sack.

"You said that boy was stalking you. What's his name?"

"Wendell. Maybe that was too strong a word. Louise, he's like me. He has no one in his life except his uncle." She pictured Wendell's sad face, like a scared child when she'd spoken to him. To see those eyes filled with pain and fear struck a chord in her. She had almost given him a hug.

"How is that like you?"

"I have no living relative except my aunt. I wouldn't want anyone taking her away from me."

"But you're not taking his uncle away from him."

"I know, but he's sensitive. Perhaps he perceives it that way."

"I hope you set him straight."

Jasmine nodded. "I think I have." Wendell was harmless. He wouldn't do anything foolish. Then he'd really risk losing Uncle Monte.

Louise was silent for a few minutes.

"How's the career hunt going?"

Jasmine was relieved that Louise changed the subject. Louise barely looked at her, though, instead eyeing the men at the bar.

"Fine. Researching where to go back to school is a lot of work. I found some good programs here and there. Florida is an option."

"You would go back there?"

"I have good memories of my undergraduate years."

Louise raised an eyebrow. "Going back for a master's is not the same party-party atmosphere of your undergraduate years."

"I don't presume it is," Jasmine said as her chest tightened. She wiped her hand along her skirt and took a sip of wine.

It would be an enormous commitment. Going back to school meant cutting back on her business or delegating more responsibility. It also meant making the decision whether to temporarily leave Portsmith or to get certified here.

So many things needed to be considered. Her aunt Harriet and the distance placed between them if she chose to go away. The house. Martha. Keeping a hand in her business while doing master-level coursework.

*I have to choose and do it quickly.*

# CHAPTER TWELVE

The chime of the doorbell took her by surprise. Jasmine peered through the peephole.

*Oh, no.*

With some hesitation, she opened the door.

"I'm sorry to disturb you so late," Monte said. His tall frame backlit by the streetlight, just the sight of him made her heart race.

Jasmine had no idea why he visited and wasn't certain she wanted to invite him inside. Having him at her doorstep was dangerous. "What's wrong?"

"I want to apologize to you for Wendell's behavior."

Her heart pounded in her chest. It would be daring to invite him in. She couldn't resist his charm. Jasmine stepped aside. "Please, come in."

They stood in the vestibule. Jasmine didn't want to get too comfortable. Yet. She closed the door on the chilly night air.

"Yeah, what was that all about?"

Monte sighed. "Wendell's insecure. Alone. No living

relatives aside from me. He's—" Monte spread his arms, as though searching for the right words.

"Oversensitive," Jasmine said for him.

"Yeah, something like that."

"And a borderline stalker."

"I don't know if I'd call him that," Monte said. His words were soft, his voice deep. Alluring.

Jasmine crossed her arms. "He drove by my house repeatedly. What do you call that behavior, Monte?"

Monte nodded. "You're right."

"As his only family, what kind of help are you getting him?"

Monte glanced at the parlor. "Can we sit?"

Jasmine nodded and led him into the small room off the vestibule. Monte sat on a sofa and Jasmine on a chair next to it.

"I've been in a little bit of denial about that. He needs help. Since my wife died, I've been blinded to some of the other problems around me. Wendell is one of them."

With sincerity in his voice, he opened up to her in a way he hadn't before. Her heart went out to him.

"Problems can be fixed, Monte."

"And I should start with my own. Jasmine, I could have used some help myself after my wife died. I didn't, and that prolonged the grieving period. As for Wendell...I've been reluctant to push him to get help when I failed to do the same."

"What do you think his problem is?"

"Oh, I know what it is. Abandonment issues. At least,

that's what my late wife told me." Monte paused, as though struggling for words. "When she first told me this story, it broke my heart. It's a little difficult to repeat."

"Can I get you something to drink? I'd like to hear this." Jasmine stood.

"Sure."

She poured two glasses of sherry she kept in a decanter and handed him one.

"Thank you."

Alcohol was the last thing she needed in his presence.

"When Wendell was a small boy, whichever foster parent he'd been dumped on at the time had taken him to an orphanage. Wendell wouldn't get out of the car. Someone from the orphanage came out and baited him with a toy. Wendell's caregiver, if that's the right word, hopped in the car and pulled away from the curb. He'd left Wendell on the sidewalk with a bag of clothes and little else."

*No wonder the kid's always on edge.*

"That's where Ellie found him years later, and the person at the home who'd baited Wendell told her that story in tears. Ellie set him up with a decent family until he turned sixteen and became emancipated."

Moisture had welled in Monte's eyes. Wendell wasn't even a blood relative of his, yet Monte cared for him as though he were. Jasmine leaned forward and squeezed his knee, causing it to jerk slightly.

"It's not too late. For either of you."

His hand slid over hers and her body shivered. Why had she opened the door and allowed him in?

She'd said her goodbyes at Brookhaven, and tonight he'd walked right into her life again. His fingers clasped around hers and sent ripples of pleasure to her tingling lady parts.

"I won't see you tomorrow," Monte said.

"That's for the best." How could she think about tomorrow with him sitting in her parlor now?

"I know we discussed giving it some time." Monte's gaze locked on hers. His serious expression made him more desirable.

"We didn't discuss it. I stated it." Her cheeks burned.

Monte nodded. "Was it wrong of me to come here?"

"Not at all. I appreciate what you said about Wendell." The heat in her core made it uncomfortable for her to pretend she didn't want him right now. She wanted him so badly she had become light-headed.

Monte knelt before her. "Tell me to go, and I'll go." His hands glided along her thighs.

*That touch.*

Jasmine's body surged and moisture pooled between her legs. Ah, his touch could do so much. The slightest gesture had her craving more.

Monte's gaze avoided hers as he bent over and kissed her skin. Her thighs tensed when his lips pressed against them. His fingers kneaded her flesh as his lips roamed farther up her leg, toward her heat. Fire raged in her core. When he reached her panties, his fingers slipped underneath and gently pulled them down.

Once they were out of the way, his mouth found her

mound, and his tongue slid between her folds. Jasmine's nails dug into her palms as the intense pleasure took over. She wanted to run, retreat to the sanctuary of a hot bath, but she didn't. He'd done the same thing to her in New Orleans, and she wanted it again.

Around and around, his tongue darted, and she squirmed. The wetness inside her passage increased. She wanted him. His thumb rubbed her nub and the warmth rushed through her body. So close, she clutched his muscular shoulders and held on.

"Monte," she whispered.

"Mmmm," he said from his place beneath her legs.

His tongue licked her insides and his thumb swirled around her pearl. Spasms of ecstasy surged through every part of her. Jasmine craved what they'd had that night long ago. How could she have been so foolish to resist him all week?

*This is what I want.*

Jasmine clenched her teeth and dug her nails into him as the waves of pleasure began.

Monte glided his tongue out of her channel. His mouth sucked on her nub.

"Oh," she cried as the orgasm racked her body, making it shake and writhe.

Monte grabbed her to hold her still. If he hadn't, she feared she would jump out of her chair and fall to the floor from light-headedness. Wave after wave surged through her body, and she struggled to regulate her breath.

*Monte.*

He'd done it again, as he had so many times that first night. Never had a man held such power in bringing her pleasure. His mouth, his touch, every part of him served her needs.

And he was capable of so much more. What had happened just now was nothing. Not even an appetizer compared to what he could do.

Jasmine closed her eyes and allowed her body to go limp as she leaned back in the chair. Monte rested his cheek against her thigh and held her.

Why now? How could she be so vulnerable to him again? Moments like this would lead to more and more, and she wasn't sure she could handle it all right now. She sat still, breathing deeply, hoping that when she opened her eyes, he'd be gone.

Of course, he wasn't.

"Monte," she whispered.

"I know," he said without looking up. "I know." He got up from the floor and rested his hands on her thighs.

She ran her fingers along his smooth, bald scalp, and he gazed up at her. The ache between her legs returned, and Jasmine couldn't turn back now.

"Come upstairs, Monte."

*Surrender. Let it happen.*

She climbed the stairway to the second floor, knowing the whole time his gaze was on her ass. She led the way not because it was her house and he wouldn't know where to go, but because she wanted him staring at her butt.

When she reached her bedroom, she didn't bother

turning on any lights. The illumination from the hallway sufficed. Jasmine removed her clothing without looking at him. She didn't have to look. His hands were on her, roving up and down her body.

He stood behind her, and his lips brushed against her neck. That small gesture sent chills through her body. His large hands caressed her belly and down between her legs, and his fingers entered her.

"Monte." She didn't want to cry his name but couldn't help it.

*It's happening again.*

She arched her head back and he kissed her throat while his fingers probed her heat. A year of loneliness in bed, and now Monte was back. The wetness between her legs increased, and she ached for more of him. Not just his fingers—she wanted his hard dick.

The movement of his fingers increased, and he showered her neck with kisses. With his free hand, he pinched her nipple.

She came again, soaking his fingers with her wetness. How much longer could she hold off? She wanted him inside her.

"Monte," she said, cursing herself for being so vulnerable. But was it vulnerable to desire a man? To want him? To enjoy the unequivocal pleasure he brought her?

He turned her body around to face him and crushed his lips against hers. She hungered for him, pushing her tongue against his. Her heart raced and head spun. Now? Could she give herself to him again?

*Monte.*

He picked her up and placed her down on the bed.

"Pull the covers off," Jasmine said and moved up on the bed, throwing back the edge of the quilt.

Monte yanked the bedspread down and removed his clothing. Jasmine gasped at the sight of his massive phallus, already rock hard. She parted her legs and placed her hands behind her head.

"Do you have any—?"

Jasmine gestured to the nightstand. "In there."

Monte opened the drawer and quickly sheathed his massive cock. The gaze, she'd recognized. That same look of lust she'd seen in him before. She opened her arms wide, and he came to her. Their lips met and his hardness pressed against her thigh.

"Don't hold back," she whispered.

He didn't. Monte pulled her legs up, rested her ankles on his shoulders, and thrust into her. She cried out and, in that moment, was transported back to the hotel in New Orleans. On her back, legs up, taking him all night long.

The eleven months that had elapsed vanished. It was as though the night together in New Orleans was just last night. He stimulated her sweet pearl as he hammered into her, sending her into another loud, bed-shaking climax. Waves of ecstasy rushed though her, bringing the release she needed. Her nails dug into his triceps, and he pushed into her harder.

Within minutes, Monte exploded with his own release, and he collapsed onto her. Even with the loud groan that escaped her, she wanted him there. On her. In her. With her. And this time, she wasn't letting him go.

Her hands glided along his back, which had broken out into a sweat. Her own breathing now regulated, she waited for him to catch up. Once he did, she held him close to her and closed her eyes.

An indeterminable amount of time passed. Jasmine's eyes fluttered open, and Monte now lay by her side, holding her in his big arms. She shifted her position, and his erection pressed against her naked flesh.

He groaned and his large hands roamed over her body, and the familiar ache returned between her legs.

*I can't resist him.*

She pulled him onto her and parted her legs, and his hardness throbbed against her. Monte reached for another condom and quickly rolled it on his massive hardness. The burning heat in her core became too intense.

"Do it, Monte."

He entered her, and his girth stretched her. She cried out and held on to his back as he rocked back and forth into her, giving her the release she needed. Knowing she wouldn't have to face him tomorrow, she let go with wild abandon.

She clawed his back and cried out his name as she'd done in that south Louisiana hotel room last year. There wasn't any holding back now. Deep, repressed desire had taken over, and she enjoyed every minute of it.

Her face flushed and her body shook with another climax of pleasure. Monte didn't let up until his own powerful release. They both drifted off to sleep.

When she woke, Jasmine sniffed the scent of sex in the air. She snuggled against his chest. His strong arm was draped around her shoulder, and she smiled at the beating of his heart. She enjoyed his company, even in silence, save for his deep breathing.

*He's still asleep.*

The stillness and the quiet comforted her, at least until she became restless. Her hand absently slipped down his treasure trail, and his manhood swelled. Although she'd barely brushed against it, his cock grew larger. She gingerly slid her hand along its length, trying to gauge its size, and squeezed it when his phallus throbbed.

Monte's breathing remained deep and his dick grew stiff in her hand. She didn't dare move. She wanted to see it, but the sheet draped it. His huge dick danced in her hand.

*No time like the present to be bold.*

She carefully slid the sheet away from his waist. He didn't stir, and his cock pulsed.

*What if he's just pretending to be asleep?*

It hardly mattered. He wouldn't object. Jasmine gently stroked his thick shaft, and it jumped at her touch. It stood straight up, pointing right at her, giving her a perfect view of its ample girth. It bucked against her soft flesh. She stared at it, about to make her move.

*Okay, here it goes.*

Monte stirred and placed his hand on the back of her head, and she took him into her mouth.

He groaned, and the thick mushroom head of his dick tasted of sex. She slid down his shaft an inch or two farther.

Monte moved his hand away from her head, and Jasmine stroked his dick as her lips glided up and down. His manhood quaked with release as she satisfied him.

His breathing was labored afterward, and Jasmine moved her head up so it leaned against his shoulder. He held her close, and she waited for his breathing to regulate. He pressed his lips against hers, and a bolt of panic raced through her.

*What does my mouth taste like after sucking his dick?*

His tongue explored hers, and he reached between her legs and rubbed her mound. She wriggled against him, aroused by his touch. He moved his head between her legs, and his tongue darted over her folds. Once he found her soft pearl, she shuddered from another intense orgasm.

After another round, he kissed her at the door and left for work.

*It happened again.*

One-night stands from a town far away on a night long ago weren't supposed to repeat themselves. But it had happened last night. Her body didn't lie to her. Every part of her fulfilled, just as that night last year.

Irresistible didn't begin to describe him. Once she'd opened that door to him last night, there wasn't any question what would happen. She'd wanted him, and she'd had him. Her body rippled with satisfaction, like that night last December. He'd done it again. He'd worked the same magic on her and left her more satisfied than ever.

Conflicting emotions raced through her. Of course she wanted him. Who wouldn't want the best sex ever to repeat itself? But then, there was the reality of waking up the next morning and going on with the day.

*Will I see him again?*

# CHAPTER THIRTEEN

Monte sat in his office unable to focus. Monday morning he'd gotten in early, having slept little the night before. After he'd left Jasmine's, he'd run home, showered, and gotten to work. But he couldn't concentrate—not after last night.

Her sweet, fresh scent embedded in his senses, he couldn't stop thinking about her. The softness of her flesh. The warmth of being inside her. He reached for a tissue and blotted his brow. How could he get any work done?

Last week, the minute he'd walked into room twenty-six and seen Jasmine standing there, he'd known it would happen again. The indiscretion he'd had with her last year had, at the time, seemed like a result of too much alcohol. But that wasn't it at all. She was the most irresistible woman he'd met since his wife, and now, Jasmine had walked into his life again.

The heaviness in his heart along with his sullen mood indicated one thing. Guilt. As much as he fought it, guilt still plagued him for being with another woman. If he had to move on from anything, it was that.

How could he explain it to Jasmine? Or would he? Perhaps none was needed. They'd done what they'd both known was inevitable. Maybe it would be another eleven months before they'd meet again.

*Who am I kidding?*

**

Jasmine stared at the exterior of the school where she'd been assigned. A bit run-down, Vista Terrace Middle School needed a paint job, for one. And a good window washing. Her heart sank as she entered the building.

*Maybe this isn't for me?*

She wasn't doubting herself and her ability to serve children but rather doubting her ability to tolerate how an education system with billions of dollars pumped into it every year had schools so shabby.

The lobby had an odd smell—old and musty like a relic from the past.

"I'm Jasmine Landers, here to sub today," she announced.

"Sign in, then have a seat," a nondescript office clerk droned.

Jasmine signed in.

*Why am I having a seat?*

She sat on an uncomfortable and not-so-sturdy wooden bench. She glanced around the office at a bunch of yellowed posters hanging on the wall. Some of them looked like they had been there for decades. Stacks of papers stood in sloppy piles on the receptionist's desk. Pens and pencils were scattered on the desk and floor. The phone—covered with sticky notes.

How could they get any work done in such a messy environment? A steady stream of staff members filed in, signed the log, and were gone without a word. After a couple of bells, Jasmine had been sitting there for quite some time, well after the start of classes.

"Excuse me," Jasmine said.

No one looked up.

"What am I waiting for?"

Finally, a clerk glanced up at her. "Miss Hawthorne has to meet you. She doesn't allow anyone on her campus she hasn't met."

Jasmine assumed Miss Hawthorne was the principal. In a few minutes, the door to her office opened. One of the clerks jumped to her feet. "A new sub is here today, ma'am."

The clerk ushered Jasmine into the office.

Miss Hawthorne sat behind a large desk. For some reason, Jasmine didn't sit down until invited to do so.

"Good morning," the woman said warmly but with a false note. It came across as forced. "I'm Claire Hawthorne, principal of Vista Terrace. What is your name?"

"I'm Jasmine Landers. Mr. Whitney sent me here."

"Yes, I know." Miss Hawthorne smiled with that same false note. "Please, sit down."

Jasmine took a seat in a chair opposite Miss Hawthorne's desk. The principal had a large frame and wore a salmon-colored designer suit. She must have had it custom-tailored for her size. A woman of about forty, she wore her hair pulled back and tied with a scarf.

"Where have you subbed before?"

"Brookhaven."

"That's it?" Hawthorne seemed surprised.

"Yes, I'm new to substitute teaching."

"Brookhaven is a small school, but I'm sure you'll do just fine here. I had one of the staff hold the class for you so I could meet you. You're in room one-fourteen. Have a good day, Miss Landers."

Miss Landers took that as her cue to stand up.

"Thank you, ma'am. It was nice to meet you."

Miss Hawthorne nodded.

Jasmine left the office and started on the search for room one-fourteen. As she started down a corridor, most classrooms had their doors open. That was odd since the noises filtered into the hallway.

"Stop talking, ladies, stop talking!"

Jasmine turned her head. A short, blonde woman who looked fresh out of college. What made matters worse, her style of dress was girlish, making her look even younger. From what Jasmine could see, the class was all girls, and they ignored the teacher. She doubted that rowdy group would stop talking just because the young neophyte said so.

As she passed another room, a child struggled with reading. A large, imposing woman with her hair twisted into a tight bun stood by the student's desk. "Sound it out!" the woman demanded.

Eventually, Jasmine found one-fourteen.

"Good luck," the staffer said as she breezed by Jasmine and made a quick getaway. Jasmine was left staring at a classroom that could only be described as chaos. She managed a smile as she wrote her name on the board. The students appeared indifferent. They talked amongst themselves, and the staff member who had held the class hadn't given them anything to do.

The vibe from this class was completely different. The kids were a few years older than her class at Brookhaven, boys and girls, and they basically ignored her. Jasmine had gotten advice about trying out different classrooms. So different. Worlds apart from Brookhaven.

She didn't know where to begin, as they were so loud. A sub folder sat untouched on the table. The staff member who'd held the class hadn't done anything. Jasmine picked up the folder and leafed through it.

*Worksheets.*

As much as she didn't consider that teaching, she quietly walked up and down each aisle and placed a worksheet on each student's desk. Oddly, that quieted them down.

*Maybe just to keep them busy this morning.*

By lunchtime, Jasmine had a headache. She'd managed to restore some peace to the class, but it was a constant struggle. They loved to talk, and their second love was procrastination.

Jasmine dropped into a chair in the teachers' lounge and drank her bottled water. She found the ibuprofen in her purse and swallowed two of the tablets.

Another woman in the lounge appeared to be having the same kind of day. She was struggling through an overstuffed purse but coming up empty-handed. Jasmine recognized the purse as one of her own designs. How could this woman could afford one on a teacher's salary?

*That's so stuck-up. I shouldn't assume.*

"May I help you?" Jasmine asked.

The woman looked up. "Oh, I'm trying to find a couple of those myself. I just can't find my bottle."

Jasmine got up and offered her the ibuprofen. "Here, you can have this bottle."

"Oh, no, I just need two...or three," the woman responded.

She took the bottle from Jasmine, awkwardly opened it, and popped three pills into her mouth. She washed them down with water.

"Thank you." She smiled.

"You're welcome. I'm Jasmine Landers."

"Maureen Howard. Nice to meet you." The woman extended her hand, and Jasmine took it. Jasmine glanced into the woman's handbag, a cluttered mess.

"Do you use the pockets on the side?" Jasmine asked. "I mean the ones on the inside lining."

Maureen shook her head. "No, I am so used to just dumping stuff in there and forgetting to clean it out."

"You can organize your bag much better with these. There are several compartments, and you'll be able to find stuff easier."

"You have one of these?" Maureen asked.

"I have several," Jasmine answered.

A light bulb must have gone off in Maureen's head. "Jasmine Landers. I didn't make the connection when you said your name because of this darned headache. What the heck are *you* doing here?"

"Substitute teaching," Jasmine answered.

"You picked one heck of a school," Maureen whispered. "I got transferred here, and after two months…" She let her voice trail off, looking up at the overhead intercom. Her whisper dropped even lower. "Sometimes the office staff will listen in."

Jasmine raised a brow. "Really?"

Maureen nodded.

That was what happened in public education? Jasmine learned more and more each step of the way. Brookhaven had its bully. Apparently Vista Terrace had its spies.

Lunch was almost over, and she hadn't even taken a bite of her sandwich yet. She ate as much of it as she could, knowing she would need the strength to get through the day.

As Jasmine signed out for the day, the clerk held out a piece of paper. "You have a message, Miss Landers."

Jasmine glanced at the paper and shoved it into her purse.

"Thank you," Jasmine said as she hurried out the door.

She was exhausted. The class had drained her, and Jasmine had only one thing on her mind—taking a nap. She wanted to go home and flop onto the bed. Jasmine slipped behind the wheel of her Lexus and took a deep breath as she pulled out of the parking lot.

When she remembered the note, she was lying facedown in bed. One shoe was dangling from her foot and the other had already fallen to the floor. Her purse was also on the floor, so she weakly reached for it. *Call Calvin Whitney,* the note read, followed by his number. What did he want? She had his number saved in her phone, so it was easy to find.

"Miss Landers, I was hoping you would call back. You're just in time. "

"For what?" Jasmine asked.

"Just in time for me not to call anyone else. Mrs. Cage came back to work today but was in a lot of pain. We let her go early so she could see her doctor, and it appears she needs surgery. Would you go back to Brookhaven tomorrow?"

"Certainly, Mr. Whitney," Jasmine mumbled.

"Good. The boys will be happy to see you. Don't worry about Vista Terrace. I'll find someone for that assignment."

*That's a relief.*

Jasmine gripped her phone. Her face flushed and a rush of excitement sent shivers through her.

*Monte.*

She'd see him again, in those sharp Givenchy shirts and silk ties. But more important, she'd be in close proximity to him.

*Can I handle it?*

# CHAPTER FOURTEEN

Tuesday morning, Jasmine parked her car in front of Brookhaven Elementary. The vibrations through her body had already started, and she hadn't stepped out of her car yet. The ache between her legs had increased as soon as she pulled into the lot.

With her hand shaking, she opened the door and emerged from her Lexus. They'd be together again. Under the same roof. Temptations that shouldn't happen on the job.

*Had he remembered my name, he could have tracked me down. Professed his undying lust for me.*

Jasmine steadied herself on her impractical high heels and smoothed her skirt. Her heart pounded in her chest as she approached the stairway. Her own desire for Monte filled her to the point that she questioned if she'd make it through the day.

It was early. Jasmine had a knack for punctuality.

The main office was silent and empty except for Monte. She spotted him sitting behind his desk, facing his computer monitor, the V-shape of his back evident since he'd removed his jacket.

Jasmine's hand trembled as she signed the substitute login sheet. When she went to replace the pen, it dropped from her sweaty fingers and clattered on the counter. Monte glanced up from his computer screen and met her gaze.

"Good morning," he said.

"Morning," she mumbled, clutched her handbag, and scurried out of the office.

Jasmine climbed the stairway as quickly as she could in her poor choice of shoes and was out of breath by the time she'd made it to her classroom. It was locked.

*Dammit. The perils of being early.*

She collapsed against the door and caught her breath. Not the best way to start the morning. Her heart still palpitated from the things she shouldn't be thinking.

The clanking of a key ring sounded behind her.

Somehow, without turning around, Jasmine was certain it wasn't the custodian.

"May I help you?"

She turned, and there he stood. Tall, dark, and gorgeous. Monte dangled his keychain in front of him.

"The door's locked." Jasmine's voice was barely above a whisper.

"I know. You beat Wallace this morning. You beat the whole staff, actually—except me. Why so early?"

"It's my nature."

Monte approached her, his shiny dress shoes echoing on the linoleum in the silence of the empty hallway. His large hands dwarfed the ring of keys.

Jasmine wished she could be anywhere else now. Suddenly, it was like one hundred degrees. Her face burned and her breath became labored.

The key inserted into the lock, and then Monte met her gaze as he turned it and the door clicked. He pushed it open for her but did not move from his position by the doorway.

"Thank you," Jasmine murmured.

She made a mental note to herself never to be early again. The pleasant fragrance of his cologne was evident as she slid past him. Her handbag dropped from her hand onto a table by the door, and she turned to face Monte.

The look in his eyes made her core surge with heat.

Monte closed the door and approached her.

Now on fire, her body shivered with want and need.

She clutched his arm for support. "Monte, why?"

"You want what I want." His plump lips pursed after he spoke.

Jasmine nodded and squeezed his arm.

Monte leaned toward her and pressed his lips against hers.

Moisture pooled between her legs and her knees wavered. She pushed her tongue into his and he tasted of peppermint.

His arms snaked around her waist, and she was grateful for the support. She threw her other arm around his neck and returned his kisses in full force. The torturous denial and smutty thoughts came to a head.

Her body quivered as his hands roamed all over her, up and down her back, through her full-bodied hair, and around her ass. The ache between her legs became unbearable as she rubbed herself against him.

Monte's hand reached beneath her skirt, and she whimpered. Now, she'd get the release she craved. His fingers rubbed against her panties, already moist with desire.

"Monte." She said his name as she had so many times during sex.

"Baby," he whispered. His fingers moved under her panties and into her heat.

Moans of ecstasy escaped her as she hooked both arms around him.

His large fingers slid into her slick heat as his thumb rubbed her sweet pearl.

"Monte."

His lips roamed along her throat and up to her ear. The flicker of his tongue sent more waves of excitement through her. "Enjoy it," he said into her ear.

The rumbles from deep within her signaled the onset of her orgasm. His fingers thrust in and out of her wetness, and his thumb made her pearl swell.

"Monte!" She cried his name as she came close.

"Do it, baby," he whispered close to her.

Her body quaked in climax, and her nails dug into his shirt. For a moment, the room went dark and she feared she'd pass out. The waves of pleasure rocked her body, and she came with his fingers deep inside her.

She buried her head in the nape of his neck and held him tightly. One of his strong arms supported her while the other remained between her legs. After a moment, she collected herself.

"Monte, we can't—"

"It's okay."

Monte removed his fingers from her soaked insides and placed them into his mouth.

Jasmine turned away from him and tried to fix her tussled clothing and then sat down before she fell. Her legs had grown weak and she didn't trust her balance.

"Have a good day. The kids are gonna be thrilled to see you."

Jasmine nodded.

Monte left her alone and she badly craved water. That would mean heading downstairs to the teachers' lounge, and she hadn't the energy right now. A box of tissues sat on the desk, and she reached for one, blotting her face with it.

It had to happen. Career path aside, she wanted him. The time was now.

She gazed at her handbag sitting across the room. As much as she wanted to go for it, her legs were like lead.

"Good morning, Miss Landers. Good to see you again."

Jasmine glanced over to the doorway. Wallace smiled at her.

"Good morning, Wallace."

"Didn't expect you back so soon."

"Apparently Mrs. Cage wasn't well yesterday?"

"Something like that. See you beat me to the classroom."

*I also had an orgasm.*

"Yes, Dr. Davis unlocked the door for me."

"I hope Mrs. Cage didn't mess up the room. You kept it so tidy last week."

"Thanks. I haven't had a chance to look around yet. I'm a bit tired this morning."

"Anything I can do for you?"

"If you don't mind, could you hand me that bag by the door?"

Wallace carried her handbag to her.

"Thank you, Wallace." Jasmine reached inside for her hairbrush.

"Have a good day, Miss."

*I just did.*

"You, too." As she ran the brush through her hair, she hoped Wallace hadn't noticed how flushed her face must be. A quick glance at the clock—still had time before the students arrived. She fixed her hair and tossed the brush back into her bag.

Jasmine descended the stairway to the teachers' lounge and drank some cool water. Nothing could douse the fire Monte had lit within her, but she sure as hell had to try.

"You're looking mighty cheery this morning."

Jasmine froze. It was Albertson, smug and condescending as always. Administrators didn't usually come into the teachers' lounge, but he had entered with Dana right behind him.

"What's that supposed to mean?" Jasmine asked.

"You've got color in your cheeks."

*Oh, shit. Don't tell me he—*

"Doesn't she?" Albertson turned to Dana.

Dana shrugged. "I don't see anything different." Dana shoved her lunch into the fridge and left the room quickly.

"You can't stay away from Brookhaven, can you?"

Jasmine ignored his comment and drank more of her water.

"There's got to be something keeping you here."

"I'm just a sub," Jasmine said, tossing her cup into the trash. "I'll be gone before you know it."

"Not soon enough for me." Albertson's scowl matched his tone.

A chill ran through Jasmine. Having a petty nemesis wasn't something she needed. Especially one as creepy as Albertson. Did he know something about her and Monte? Or was that her own paranoia.

As Jasmine left the room, she was certain his gaze bored into her back. For some odd reason, he targeted her, and she couldn't understand why. Standing up to an administrator wasn't a crime, and she could hardly be a threat to him.

She crept back up the stairs to the second floor, each step heavy with the weight of her orgasm-racked body. As good as it was, it wasn't exactly the way she'd intended on beginning her morning. And certainly not in the classroom.

What if they'd been caught? Albertson could have gotten here early enough to hear or see something.

When Jasmine reached her room, she glanced at the blinds. They were closed, so no one could have seen anything. She opened them and let in some of the morning sunshine.

The bell rang and her eleven boys filed in, elated to see her. Smiles, hugs, and high fives started her morning, and she was grateful to be here. She'd found her place. Serving these children was her mission.

The morning breezed by, and the boys were filled with questions. Jasmine beamed. This reassured her that she'd made the right decision.

Back in the teachers' lounge for lunch, Jasmine crunched on the pickle that accompanied her sandwich. After she sat alone for a few minutes, Dana came in to retrieve her lunch from the fridge.

"Hey, how's it going?" Dana asked.

"Great. Happy to see the boys again."

"They're happy to see you, I'm sure." Dana grabbed her sack lunch. "Can I join you?"

"Please do."

Dana pulled up a chair. "What was all that business with Albertson this morning?"

Jasmine shook her head. "I don't know. He seems to have it in for me."

"But you're not even on staff here. It's not like he has to deal with you all year."

"You'd know more about him than me."

Dana nodded. "Oh, he's an odd one—the old sourpuss. Been bounced around from school to school. I wouldn't be surprised if the district moved him someplace else next year."

"I'm sure you'll all be glad to see him go."

"Yeah, they should send him over to Vista Terrace. Miss Hawthorne would make minced meat out of him."

Jasmine found it odd that Dana brought up Vista Terrace. No one knew she had been there yesterday except Mr. Whitney. After this morning, Vista Terrace seemed like an eternity ago.

"How long has Albertson worked for the district?" Jasmine asked.

"Oh, umpteen years. You know Portsmith. They never get rid of anyone—they just move 'em around from school to school."

"He doesn't seem very compassionate toward the children."

Dana shook her head. "Oh, no. I don't know why he got into education." She peeled her over-ripened banana. "Then again, I don't know why a lot of folks get into education these days."

"I'm headed that way. I'm going back to college to do my alt cert."

"Bless your heart," Dana said. "They need more folks like you." Dana's expression beamed. Her complexion had a pinkish hue, although that was probably from the makeup she wore.

"How long have you been teaching?"

Dana rolled her eyes. "Don't ask. That would give away my age. I've been doing this for a long time."

"What keeps you going?"

Dana cocked her head to the side. "My mortgage." She let out a hearty laugh.

"Oh, Dana. I found this is my mailbox." Jasmine held up the flyer printed on yellow paper with brown trim. It had something to do with a Thanksgiving show.

"We do that every year. It's right before Thanksgiving break, and all the parents are invited."

"Do I have to do anything?"

Dana nodded. "Sure you do. You have to put a little something together with your class. We all do. It doesn't have to be long. Five minutes is usually enough."

"Something like what?"

"Could be a play, a song." Dana cocked her head to one side. "A reading of some sort, a tribute, a biography, a holiday-themed thing…"

Jasmine frowned.

"Oh, come on." Dana smiled. "It's a whole lot of *fuuuuuun!*"

"Yeah, it'll be awesome," Jasmine said, not at all convinced.

"Let me know if I can help you with anything," Dana offered. "My class is going to do a presentation on the topography and weather conditions at the first Thanksgiving."

Jasmine couldn't help but wonder how topography and weather conditions could possibly be *fuuuuuun*. She would discuss it with the boys and include them so they were a part of the decision-making.

Dana glanced at that clock. "They sure don't give us much time to eat."

She said the word time with a southern drawl, dragging it out as *tiiiiime*. Her strawberry-blond locks shook when she spoke. The older woman's warmth comforted Jasmine in contrast to some of the cold characters she'd met at Brookhaven.

After lunch, Jasmine contemplated grabbing her bag and running out the door to her car. She couldn't work with Monte, not after what had happened in the morning. It wasn't right for them to be here together, doing things in a classroom that were best left for the bedroom.

They were two adults driven by lust. Neither one of them would get a good grade for self-control. Jasmine needed to pull herself together. She made it through the school day with soaked panties, a flushed complexion, and wobbly knees.

How could she get any work done under these conditions? She needed to concentrate on educating children, not on basking in the afterglow of an early-morning orgasm.

She walked back upstairs, realizing that she should have some ideas to offer. After all, it was her job as the teacher to initiate discussion. She looked at the flyer and shook her head. Her mind was coming up blank. Maybe they could create a dance? They were certainly a lively enough group.

The bell rang, and DaShon was already at the door. Sometimes, when all the other kids were at lunch, Jasmine had noticed him lurking in the hallway with his back against the wall as though holding it up. He sat down quietly, and the other boys soon followed.

"Can we have a light afternoon?" Demetrius asked. That was his code for not wanting to do any work.

"How about we start off light?" Jasmine offered. "Let's talk about this Thanksgiving event."

Groans filled the classroom.

"Are you serious, Miss L?"

"They got you doin' that, too?"

"Do we have to?"

Jasmine could see she had a tough crowd. "What did you do last year?"

"Our class read some stupid poem," Tyrone volunteered.

"And we just took turns reading from a book," Jamal said.

Clearly their teachers last year hadn't challenged them. With Dana choosing topography, Jasmine could see there was a lack in creative thinking at Brookhaven.

"Okay." Jasmine scanned the room. "What would you *like* to do?"

"Stay home," Jamal shot back.

Everyone laughed. Jasmine couldn't help but smile. She would prefer to be at home rather than Old Portsmith on the last night before Thanksgiving break.

"What are some things you enjoy doing?" Jasmine asked.

"Play basketball," Corey answered.

Jasmine nodded. "You like to move around. You're very good on your feet. How about a dance?"

The boys looked skeptical.

"What kind of dance?" LeRoy asked. "We're not gonna fox trot."

Amid the roars of laughter, Jasmine was impressed they remembered that word from their discussions of *Tender Is the Night*.

"Let's do hip-hop," Jamal said.

Jasmine clapped her hands. "Good idea. Let's do it."

"You would let us?"

"Yes, Jamal, I would."

"Dayum, they never let us do that before!"

"Well, guess what? We won't tell them. If they ask, we'll just say we're doing a performance. Now all we have to do is find the right music."

At least she had made some strides in getting her boys excited about the event. She had to be there for them.

With Thanksgiving break coming up, she had to plan for the weekend. She'd spend Thanksgiving Day with Aunt Harriet, as she always did. But then? Maybe she'd give Yvonne a call. Jasmine hadn't visited her college BFF in quite some time.

Yvonne, like herself, had opened her own business. Cosmetology was Yvonne's area of expertise. She'd done well for herself, building up a loyal clientele.

A weekend trip to Florida might be a good idea.

Close to the end of the school day, she received a text from Monte. *Please join me for drinks at the Connor.*

Jasmine put her phone in her handbag and contemplated the message.

*What now?*

# CHAPTER FIFTEEN

Dark, warm, and somewhat quiet, the lounge of the Connor Hotel had soft, unobtrusive music playing. Pleased with his selection, Monte carefully selected a classy location after that impromptu moment of passion in the classroom. He sat at a cozy booth for two, sipping a drink.

He hoped she'd approve of the setting, although he didn't feel the need to impress her. Just help her feel more comfortable. He couldn't deny the tension between them at Brookhaven.

*I made her come in the classroom.*

That was an act of insanity. Anyone could have walked in. Well, anyone who could have arrived at Brookhaven early. Fortunately, no one had.

*I can't control myself in my own school.*

No. What he couldn't do was control himself around Jasmine. He'd been grateful when she accepted his invitation today. After what had happened this morning, he couldn't let anther day go by without seeing her. He couldn't allow that to happen again, at least not at school. Had someone like Albertson seen them, Monte's career would be over.

Jasmine waltzed in promptly at four thirty, looking every bit the beautiful woman. Her gorgeous chestnut hair framed her soft face. He waved to her, and she returned a stunning smile. His cock swelled against his pants and his chest heaved.

Monte stood. "It's good to see you."

"It's nice to see you as well." She'd changed into a stunning black cocktail dress.

Monte guided her to a seat, and within a moment the waiter appeared with a drink.

"A cosmopolitan, ma'am." He placed the drink before her.

"Thank you."

"A change of pace." Monte raised his rocks glass.

Jasmine glanced at him and took a sip. Her glossy lips puckered against the rim of the glass.

"How did your day go?"

"Wonderful." Jasmine lowered her drink. "I was happy to see the boys. I've grown quite fond of them."

"I know."

"And yours?"

Monte frowned. "It was fine, just meeting after meeting at central office, listening to lots of talk. I would have rather remained at Brookhaven."

"How did you choose the Connor?"

"It's classy. I thought we deserved a step up from the Blooming Cactus."

She glanced around the room.

Monte couldn't take his eyes off of her. He'd made the mistake of not getting her contact info back in New Orleans, and he wasn't about to make any mistakes now. Although he'd resisted any contact with women since Ellie's passing, he couldn't resist Jasmine. That had become apparent on that long night of passion last year.

"How did your research go over the weekend?"

"Well, although I'm a little overwhelmed. I have to sort through it one evening this week, narrow things down, think of some questions I need to ask."

Monte raised his gimlet. "To your success as a teacher."

"A little premature." Jasmine lifted her glass.

Since that unforgettable moment in the classroom this morning, he couldn't shake her image from his mind. He'd had to see her again.

"I keep breaking my own rule." Monte smiled. "No talking about work outside of work."

"We're not talking about work. We're talking about a career."

He nodded. "Touché."

She had style, class, and elegance. Yet from the way she carried herself, she still held something back. Perhaps his position as principal made her uncomfortable. It was up to him to find a way to reach her.

The waiter appeared, and Monte nodded.

"Oh, no, thank you." Jasmine gestured with her hand. "I'm *not* having another."

"We have time before dinner." He winked at her.

"What dinner? You invited me here for a drink."

"One gimlet." Monte dismissed the waiter. He turned to Jasmine. "That's my surprise… Yes, ma'am. Dinner at 5:15 p.m. sharp."

"Monte, now that I'm back at Brookhaven, maybe we should wait."

"I can't wait any longer. This morning proved that."

"Someone might see us and talk."

"Let them talk. Mrs. Cage won't be absent forever. It wouldn't surprise me if she returns next week."

"Someone could have seen us this morning."

"But no one did. I know, I was wrong to do that on campus."

Jasmine's face turned pink. When she spoke, her tone was low and breathy. "It was awesome."

"Will you give me a chance?"

"That's why I'm here."

"So you'll stay for dinner?"

Jasmine nodded.

Monte leaned back. Jasmine hadn't had it easy. Maybe due to what she'd experienced at Brookhaven. Albertson had been horrible to her. She'd been assaulted by a student. But the pretty lady demonstrated strength.

Her resilience impressed him. Many subs would have bolted and never returned. Jasmine kept up the good work, day after day. She risked so much, moving from a successful career in fashion into teaching. He admired her for her courage.

When she'd walked into Brookhaven last week, he hadn't been able to believe it. He hadn't expected to see her again.

Now, she was here, with him, and he wasn't about to let her get away.

He'd spent far too much time the last two years despondent over Ellie's death. Friends encouraged him to move on but he couldn't. Not until that night in New Orleans when it had all changed. Once he'd met Jasmine, he hadn't wanted anyone else. The heat that rushed through him, the hours of pleasure, and her insatiable needs that had matched his.

*The sex is amazing.*

But that couldn't be all, could it? Or was that all he could handle?

After he finished his gimlet, Monte led Jasmine by the arm out of the lounge.

"Where are we going?"

"To dinner, of course." Monte pressed the button for the elevator. Jasmine stared at him quizzically. Monte led her inside the car.

She didn't speak on the short ride up. As he stood close to her, the fragrance of her perfume made his blood pump a bit faster.

The elevator doors opened. Monte led her out and swiped a room card. With his arm against the small of her back, Monte guided her into a suite with dinner spread out over a linen-covered table. With his fingers pressed against her, his cock stiffened even more.

\*\*

The aroma of an Italian feast filled the air around her. Hints of garlic, thyme, oregano, and basil.

"Nice ambiance." Jasmine surveyed the room.

*Romantic.*

"I'm glad you like it."

Jasmine's body tingled from his hand against her back.

"I know it's difficult with you working at Brookhaven, but Mrs. Cage will be back."

*Does he read minds, too?*

Jasmine nodded. "I heard her surgery went well."

A bolt of excitement went through her body, lighting her on fire, and she surrendered to the ambiance he'd created. She craved the warmth he gave her, night after night.

*It isn't so simple.*

They'd have a lot to talk about but tonight wasn't the time. It took a lot out of Monte to express the desire to grow, and she respected his strength and honesty.

There was so much more she could say. Protest. Ask him to please put off evenings like these until she was out of his school building. But she couldn't offend his kindness.

"It's been so difficult after my wife…."

His pained expression touched her heart. He rarely spoke about his wife in her presence. His voice trembled as he spoke those words. Monte hadn't shown a vulnerable side. Perhaps that was what held him back emotionally. He'd reach out and then pull back.

Sexually, no pulling back. He gave it all.

They sat in silence for a moment. If Monte wanted to talk it about it, he would, but she was not about to press him.

Jasmine savored a sip of the wine he'd poured for her,

although it probably wasn't such a good idea to drink alcohol in his presence.

Again.

Another glance around the suite revealed simple and tasteful furnishings. White linen tablecloth and white candles. Gold accents around the windows. Warm bread and dipping oil. She broke off a piece of bread and dipped it into the oil.

"Delicious."

Monte nodded. "If the food's as good as this bread, we have a lot to look forward to."

Monte put his hand over hers, and her whole body went warm at his touch. She'd hoped to spend some time with Monte away from Brookhaven, and here they were.

But this wasn't the right time. Not when she had to go back and face him again in the morning. It was too awkward.

A shiver seized her entire body.

If anything, Monte exuded confidence. It had taken a great deal of effort and expense on his part to set this up. He had to be cocksure of himself to believe she'd go along with him and not bail.

If she were to steer the conversation in a different direction, she'd have to move quickly. She hadn't asked him much about his future, and took a chance.

"Monte, what's your five-year plan?" Jasmine looked at his face, and she could see the question threw him.

"My five-year plan? I'm not sure I've written one down."

"You don't have to put it in writing, but everyone thinks about where he's going to be in five years. Don't you?"

"Sure, I do. I've been in the education system fifteen

years, so I could retire in five. If I still love it, I'll stay. If I feel anything less than love for it, I'll get out."

"You love it that much?"

"Sure…that's why I'm in it. I've always wanted to be a teacher. You have to be a teacher for at least five years before you can pursue anything outside the classroom. I was a teacher for eight. In addition to the retirement check I could get in five years, I have plenty of investments and other business interests to keep me busy and financially secure."

"You've done so well outside of education that you don't really *need* to be there."

Monte nodded. "That's correct. I don't need to be there. I *choose* to."

"That's an admirable place to be in your career."

"You're doing the same in a way. You have a successful handbag business. You're pursuing education because you're drawn to it."

"Yes," she agreed. "You're right." He hit on something not often acknowledged. Teaching had chosen her, in a way. She had been drawn to it and had been easily won over by the students.

"And in five years…personally?"

Monte pressed his lips together. "That's the hard part, isn't it? Career goals are so much easier. Personally…"

Jasmine hadn't been married before and struggled with how deep she should probe into his personal life. With a deep breath, she went there.

"Does it make you uncomfortable to discuss your wife?"

"No, not anymore." There wasn't a hint of defensiveness

in his voice. "It was a long and painful struggle. When it came to an end, I felt relieved she was in a better place. But then my journey had only started."

"But you said before you hadn't really moved on."

"No. Not yet. Or not as much as I should be. I still seem to hold a lot of that in me. Not sure what that says for my future."

"What do you want?"

"To be with someone again. But I don't want to mess it up with unresolved baggage."

She nodded. She had been so young when her parents passed that she couldn't recall the grieving process she'd gone through. Some memories of that time seared her mind, while others thankfully had faded away long ago.

She hadn't really wanted to talk about his wife. There were other subjects she'd rather tackle.

"Hey, can I ask you something personal?"

"Go right ahead."

"What makes you so good in bed?"

Monte laughed out loud. "What makes you ask?"

"Your lovemaking skills are the best I've had in my life. You didn't get there by accident."

"Um..." Monte paused. "It takes two for good lovemaking. I can't do it all by myself."

"You know what I mean. How did you get so good?"

"It's very simple. I took some advice my from younger brother."

"*Younger* brother? Don't you mean older brother?"

*He's got to be putting me on.*

"No. My younger brother. Not that much younger, just a year. But he was sexually active long before I ever did anything. I was a nerd. I always wanted to be a teacher, so I always had my nose in a book while he was out chasing girls."

"So what was his advice?"

"Always be focused on pleasing the woman."

"That's it?"

"Not exactly. He gave me an explanation why."

"What?"

Monte shifted in his chair. "It's not all that interesting."

"I want to hear it." Jasmine had a hunch it would be most interesting. If he was so damned good in bed at thirty-seven, she could only image how well he'd conquered young women when he was a good fifteen to twenty years younger.

Monte grinned. "Okay. He said if you focus on your own needs, the woman's gonna spread it all over the neighborhood that you're lousy in bed. Then no one will want to date you. We grew up in a small 'hood, so the gossip was inevitable. But if you focus on *her* needs, then she'll tell every girl in town how good in bed you are, and you'll have women lined up at your door."

"Did you?" Jasmine's limbs tingled.

"No!" Monte said a little too fast. "That was my brother's job."

Monte picked up a piece of chocolate and placed it between his teeth. He leaned toward her and brushed the confection against her lips. His nose rubbed against hers, tickling her.

*Smooth.*

She nibbled on it lightly, the sweet cocoa stimulating her taste buds. His lips touched hers as he bit into the chocolate.

*Those lips.*

With a furtive gaze, he raised a single glass of the wine to her lips, and she sipped it. He pulled the glass toward himself and ran his tongue over the rim before drinking.

*What's he doing?*

He moved close to her and pressed his lips against hers. A rush of heat surged through her, and her hand dropped to his lap. Her palm brushed against his hard cock, and the desire within her couldn't wait. Warmth seared her cheeks, and a strong arm slid around her bottom and pulled her close. When he kissed her, she surrendered her tongue to his. She had Monte just where she wanted him.

*And loving every minute.*

His strong arms gripped her buttocks and hoisted her up. She inhaled sharply, her core on fire. He glided his tongue along her neck, then over one ear as she held on tightly to his back. When he moved his mouth between her breasts, she let out a soft cry.

Once lowered onto the sofa, he helped her with her dress until her breasts were exposed, and he took one of them into his mouth. He sucked on her swelling nipple and reached his hand between her legs. Waves rippled through her, and she clutched his shoulders.

The fabric of her panties provided no barrier from his roving hands. Moans were unleashed from deep within her as he rubbed her mound.

"Monte." His name came out as a breathless whisper.

He sucked on her other breast while rubbing her special spot. She cried out in pleasure, her body writhing from his touch. The hunger for him made her ache all over, an ache that throbbed deep inside her.

Almost in slow motion, Monte moved his mouth back up to hers and kissed her deeply as she approached climax. She squirmed and quivered underneath him and came from his touch. Pleasure rushed through her as she clutched his head in her hands.

Jasmine gasped to catch her breath, her body quaking from release. The room went dark for a moment as she became light-headed but quickly composed herself.

Monte helped her remove the remainder of her clothing, and she arched her back to assist him. She was naked, breathing heavily, and he quickly discarded his own clothes. His beautiful muscular body, robust hairy chest, and strong arms all beckoned to her.

*So my type.*

He hoisted her up and lowered her onto his sheathed phallus. A sharp cry followed by a long moan came from deep within her. Desire made the ache between her legs swell. She bobbed on his thickness, taking him into her wet center.

*He's so fucking good!*

He played with her nub, triggering jolts of ecstasy.

She writhed on his thick cock, so close to another release.

"Do it!" Jasmine screamed. She rocked up and down on him until she came a second time. Her nails clawed into his chest as she shook, still seated on his erection. Monte thrust deeper into her until he exploded with a loud groan. He pulled Jasmine close to him and held her tightly.

Her head spun. It was like New Orleans all over again. A hotel room. Unbridled passion. Sex that would surely last all night.

Monte had stamina like no other man.

\*\*

After an uneventful day at school and no visits from Monte, Jasmine bolted out of the building and headed to her car.

Unfortunately, Albertson blocked her path.

"Where are you going?" he asked.

"I'm on my way home, and you're in my way."

"You're not very respectful."

"I'm not on the clock. Even if I were, I'd be under no obligation to answer your prying questions. Good day, Mr. Albertson."

"Something's going on with you and Davis."

Jasmine froze. She couldn't find the words to respond. Anything she'd say would sound defensive. And the way he barked out "Davis" instead of referring to Monte by his title of Doctor was unsettling. Although others did it, too, but when Albertson spoke, it came out like spewing venom.

"What do you have to say for yourself?" The dull eyes harbored something evil, and his usually gray pallor appeared red with anger.

"Nothing, except I'm going home and you're in my way." Jasmine moved around him, although it wasn't easy with his rotund build, and made it to her car.

"Don't think I won't find out what's really going on." Albertson's voice was like fingernails on a chalkboard. "You don't hide it so well. I'll find out and I'll end both your careers. Yours before it even starts."

Jasmine shoved her key in the car door and hurried inside. After she started the car and backed out, Albertson continued to glare at her. The frightening thing was that he was in a profession to oversee children. If this was how he dealt with the adults, she cringed at how he must treat the kids.

*What does he know?*

# CHAPTER SIXTEEN

After Monte placed his phone down, he leaned back in his chair and gazed around his office. Maybe the call signaled a turning point. Lots of hard work and over a dozen years of college had led him to his current position as principal. Looking for the next opportunity was a logical step. Not only to build up retirement but for the prestige.

If it hadn't been for his doctorate degree, they probably wouldn't have considered him as seriously. He'd labored years for that paper. With his wife by his side, receiving that degree was a major milestone.

The time had come. The call had come in. Now he had to do something about it or continue to suffer in silence. Still, it wasn't an easy decision.

He turned to his computer monitor and searched for a flight to Lafayette. Having something to be excited about boosted his confidence. Not that he necessarily lacked it, but it was reassuring to have an outside district acknowledge his credentials.

After Monte booked the flight, he got ready to leave.

"Miss Johnson, I'll be out of the office Friday."

"Okay," she said without looking up from her work.

That was one thing he liked about her, she didn't need any explanation. He wished all the staff behaved like that.

When he finished what he needed to do in the office, he drove to Centerdale Cemetery.

The cool air tightened his already stoic expression and the sky had begun to darken. He stood by his wife's neatly maintained grave and waited once again for tears that never came. The years they'd been together were happy yet had raced by. Both had demanding careers and both were driven. And where had it ended up? One dead, the other painfully lonely.

He and his wife had been so consumed with success they'd allowed so much slip by. Monte went numb as he stared at her headstone, not really seeing the words. It had all become a blur.

Monte drove home and lumbered into the house. When he stared out into the darkness of the quiet, cool evening, Jasmine permeated his consciousness. He'd barely gotten a glimpse of her at school today, and when he had, she hadn't acknowledged his presence. Surely she didn't feel uncomfortable about him. Or did she?

He was haunted by pangs of guilt. Even after a year, his wife was a strong presence in this house. When he couldn't stand being in the house any longer, he grabbed his jacket and stepped outside.

Monte found Jasmine's house, but there was no answer. He wanted to see her tonight, talk to her, and make sure everything was okay. After standing outside for a few minutes, he drove away.

Jasmine could easily fill his time. He loved the way she tasted, the way she smelled. He wanted to feel her flesh and soft, wet folds. Monte shook his head.

*This is no way to think while driving.*

His grip slipped on the steering wheel from the sweat on his hands. A glance in the rearview mirror revealed moisture on his forehead as well. Ever since his wife's passing, he couldn't handle another woman. His hand trembled.

He pulled himself together. This wasn't any time to lose himself.

*She's driven.*

He wanted Jasmine in an almost painful way. She aroused him, but his feelings for her went well beyond the physical. Fiercely independent, she certainly didn't need him. The attraction between them was unquestionable. He was amazed that the staff at the school hadn't picked up on their chemistry.

*Or have they?*

He wasn't certain. No gossip had filtered back to him...yet. Monte wanted to take his relationship with Jasmine to the next level. He wasn't sure what that was yet. Honestly, he still hadn't gotten over Ellie's death.

*The next step.*

He needed to show Jasmine that he was serious about her.

*After Friday's business trip, she might want nothing to do with me.*

# CHAPTER SEVENTEEN

Jasmine stared at her laptop, reading over the guidelines again to make sure she'd understood it. She had to take two tests before she could enroll in a teacher preparation program. Since the tests had to be scheduled and were only offered on certain days, that was going to seriously stall her plans.

Suddenly, it was as though a boulder rested on her chest, and she needed to pass these two tests to move it.

"It's always something," Jasmine murmured.

"What's that, hon?" her aunt asked from her seat on the couch. Harriet sipped a cup of tea while absently flipping channels.

Jasmine abandoned the computer and sat next to Aunt Harriet.

"Even before I apply to an alt cert program, I have to pass two tests. Four, really, since the first test is three parts."

"What is alt cert?"

"Alternative certification. It's a teacher prep program for candidates who already have a bachelor's degree."

"So what kind of tests do you have to take?"

"Ugh. The first one is writing, math, and English. The second is content."

"All that before you apply?"

"They won't accept a candidate without test scores."

"That's gonna keep you busy for a while."

Jasmine frowned. "That's what I was thinking."

Already November, by the time she scheduled the tests and received her scores, the earliest she could start would be summer. Not to mention prepping for them, buying any necessary manuals, and taking the time out of her day to study. It seemed monumental.

*Oh, well. I want it, so I'll do what it takes.*

Aunt Harriet placed her teacup down. "How's your fella?"

"He's not my fella."

"Coulda fooled me. He can help you, you know."

"I don't need his help."

"Jasmine, you're stubborn. Just like your father." Harriet appeared wistful.

"And how was he stubborn?"

Harriet sighed. "He liked things done his way, and he liked to do things himself. He never asked anyone for help."

"I don't like obstacles."

"This isn't an obstacle. It's a challenge. If you're going into education, you're going to be challenged every day. Deal with it."

Jasmine pursed her lips. "I suppose so."

Aunt Harriet was right. In her short time at Brookhaven,

Jasmine dealt with challenges each day. Those challenges would probably become tougher and tougher as she immersed herself in public education.

What she had to cope with as a sub paled in comparison to what she faced as a classroom teacher. She'd taken on many responsibilities as a sub. Once she secured salaried employment, the pressure would surely increase.

*I can handle it.*

In the short time she'd been at Brookhaven, the boys had grown on her. They, more than anything else, confirmed she'd made the right decision in her career move. Now, she had to make it all happen.

"What if I don't pass the tests?"

"Are you serious?" Harriet asked. "Look around at some of the teachers out there. How hard can the tests be?"

The comment stung.

*Does Harriet have a low opinion of teachers?*

"I'm sure the tests are challenging."

"You'll be fine, Jasmine. Take the tests and move on to the next step."

The next step. Apply to colleges. Likely be interviewed. Register for courses. Pay them money. It would be fun to go back to college. And starting in the summer would be less pressure.

It had been about ten years since Jasmine earned her bachelor's degree. A lot had changed. But alt cert programs were only for those with bachelor's degrees. She'd be among peers, not undergraduates.

"Can I get you more tea?" Jasmine asked.

"Yeah. This cup's gone cold."

Jasmine picked up her aunt's cup and retreated to the kitchen.

College. More studying. Books. Tuition. It excited her. She had a goal, and it was time to pursue it. For the first time in a while, she had something to focus on. Something optimistic and meaningful.

She switched the kettle on and tossed the old teabag. Aunt Harriet's kitchen was well-stocked and had a little of everything. Ceramic canisters filled with coffee, cookies, and teabags. A bowl of cranberry potpourri. A skirt on the dishwashing liquid container to keep it from getting sticky. So many memories of childhood flooded back to her.

So many times she'd sat in the same kitchen with her parents, when she was just a small girl. Today, it meant the world to her to be in this kitchen again. Like being at home.

As a small girl, she'd stood at the kitchen counter with her mother. Her father, aunt, and guests were in the living room. Jasmine helped her mother stir some drinks on a tray. Her little fingers gripped the red plastic swizzle stick and stirred it around and around.

Jasmine ran her finger along one of the figurines on the counter. The same figurine had been there during her childhood. Her chest tightened for a minute, and she fought off the tears that came when she remembered of her parents. So many long years ago.

\*\*

Friday morning, Jasmine filled her lungs with the cool November air as she stepped out of her Lexus. A day at

Brookhaven without Monte promised to be a day without sexual tension. Apparently, he'd be absent today.

*No telling what the weekend will bring.*

Jasmine entered the building and was immediately struck by something intangible. A different vibe. Something different, but specifically what, she couldn't decipher.

When she entered the office, Miss B leaned back in her chair, yapping on her mobile phone. Jasmine signed in, and Miss B didn't give her so much as a snarl.

Teachers stood in the hallway chatting when they would normally be on duty monitoring the bus arrivals.

*Monte's gone.*

When the principal was absent, the school was a very different place indeed. Jasmine ascended the stairway to her classroom, uncomfortable with what she'd just seen. Shouldn't professionals be doing their jobs regardless of whether or not the boss was here?

Her classroom door was unlocked—at least the custodian had done his job. If the adults behaved that way when the boss was absent, how would the children act? Jasmine placed her bag down and waited for what other challenges lay ahead today.

"I see you showed up."

Jasmine's skin crawled. Albertson stood in her doorway and displayed his usual scowl.

"I would have thought since Monte wasn't here today, you wouldn't be here as well." He leaned forward when he spoke.

"What's that got to do with anything?" Jasmine's blood

boiled and her head hurt. The last thing she wanted was to have it out with Albertson this morning, but she would if he pushed her buttons.

"Considering how much time you spend together." Albertson glared at her.

Jasmine's cheeks burned and her chest tightened. She wasn't about to dignify anything he'd said. The audacity of that man enraged her.

"It isn't wise for a teacher to be spending that much time with her superiors. And it certainly doesn't look good for Monte. He could be brought up on abuse of power charges."

Jasmine's ears seared. Threats weren't something Jasmine took lightly. If Albertson tried to guilt her into staying away from Monte, what other desperate steps would he take?

"If you're so concerned about how much time principals spend with teachers, why do you spend so much time harassing me?"

"That's a strong word, Miss Landers."

"Keep it up. You'll find out how strong it is."

"That sounds like a threat."

"I don't make threats."

Albertson grimaced before he walked away.

*I knew it.*

Her fists clenched so hard she checked her palms to see if she'd nicked any skin. She'd suspected he'd been on to them, and her hunch had just been confirmed. Or had he merely baited her? Tried to get her to admit something? Call his bluff?

He had presented no evidence. Given no examples of

times he'd known they'd been together. It could be all bull.

A short time later, the students arrived. Their demeanor made her smile and reminded her of why she stayed here. They put an extra skip in her step and validated her career change. At least the boys' behavior remained consistent, although a few were still absent due to Albertson's ridiculous disciplinary measures.

Throughout her morning lessons, she kept the classroom door closed. Several times she caught Albertson peering at her through the glass window in the door. Clearly with Monte gone, Albertson behaved like king of the castle. Unfortunately, he was, in a way. If any concerns came up throughout the school day, they'd have to be addressed through Albertson.

That creepy man made her skin crawl. He'd made a target of her, and she didn't understand why. She was no threat to him or anyone else. He was merely a bully. If getting away from Brookhaven meant getting away from him, she'd be only too happy when her assignment ended.

How could an employee show up for work everyday and deal with someone like him? The stress of a job was enough without the added stress of an adult bully.

*Can I get through this day?*

# CHAPTER EIGHTEEN

Monday morning, Monte welcomed Corey back to Brookhaven. Also, the boys Albertson had placed in in-school suspension were back in the classroom. Pleased all eleven boys were here, Monte was certain that would make Jasmine's day.

The weekend had gone well. He'd had his interview with Lafayette on Friday. Spent the remainder of the weekend sightseeing around the town. Even checked out a few properties.

Something didn't feel quite right about it, but Monte chalked that up to the fear of change.

*Change.*

Badly needed after the loss of Ellie. The long, lonely nights of suffering and uncertainty provided no answers on what to do next. Now, a plum position dangled before him, one that came with the promise of a fresh start.

Maybe selling the house would be the best thing he could do. It served as a tomb of memories. Good thoughts to cherish but, at the same time, a constant reminder of what had been lost.

He glanced at the phone for a moment, knowing he could hear from them at any time today.

*Or not.*

He hadn't seen Jasmine since he'd left for the day on Thursday and ached to gaze at her beautiful features. But he'd have to wait until her break.

That was, if he could slip out of the office. He had stacks of paperwork to catch up on. Public education, with all its efforts to cram technology down the throats of students, hadn't yet gone paperless.

About an hour later, Miss Johnson poked her head into his office. "There are a couple of suits in the conference room waiting for you."

"Waiting for me? I don't have any appointments, do I?"

"No. They're from the dark tower."

Monte smirked. That was a common nickname in the district for central office. "Okay, lemme see what that's all about."

When he reached the conference room, seldom used for that purpose and mainly for storage, he recognized a couple of faces. Miss Hall from human resources and Leo Rathburn, the assistant superintendent.

"Good morning, Davis." Leo stood and shook his hand. They'd always been on relatively good terms.

Hall forced a smile but said nothing. Aloof and elitist, she seldom acknowledged Monte's existence unless she wanted something out of him. Like forcing him to give one of her cronies a job on his campus, which she'd tricked him into doing his first year as principal.

"Good morning." Monte remained standing. "I don't recall a scheduled meeting."

"It isn't." Hall finally spoke.

"Davis, my apologies for not scheduling something formally, but we needed to come by and chat with you about a concern."

"Unscheduled meetings seldom bring good news."

"We're not here with good news." Hall shifted in her chair.

Rathburn shot her a look. "I got this, Prudence."

Monte had never heard of anyone refer to her as anything other than Miss Hall. With a name like Prudence, that wasn't surprising.

"Davis, you know how people like to talk in this town…" Rathburn leaned back in his chair.

"Don't sugarcoat it," Hall snapped.

"I said I got this. You're here as a formality."

"No, I'm not here as a formality. The complaint came to me."

"What complaint?" Monte folded his arms.

"Not so much a complaint." Rathburn glanced at Hall. "But rather, a concern."

Monte, out of the corner of his eye, could swear he'd just seen Hall roll hers.

"About?"

"It was an abuse of power concern. The complaint stated…" Rathburn squinted at his notes. "Spending excessive or academically unnecessary time with a subordinate."

"I have no idea what the complaint refers to." Monte still

hadn't sat. He wasn't about to take bait from anyone.

"Concern, not complaint," Rathburn said.

"Who's the subordinate?"

"A substitute teacher," Hall said.

Now Monte wanted to roll his eyes. But refrained. "Define excessive."

"The complaint doesn't offer a definition."

"How about defining academically unnecessary?"

Hall glanced at Rathburn. "Leo?"

Rathburn put his notes down. "Like I said, this was only a concern. Not a formal complaint. So, it didn't come with those details or even specific examples. Although I did ask for examples."

"So what's the point of this impromptu meeting?"

"To make you aware of the concern so it doesn't escalate into a…"

"Formal complaint," Hall said.

"Good. Then we're done here. And if I hear any more of this nonsense without dates, times, places, pictures, video, audio recordings, or any other hard evidence"— Monte looked directly at Prudence—"tell your informant that he'll be on the receiving end of a harassment complaint from me."

Rathburn looked at Hall, his expression twisted in discomfort. Hall's frozen mask didn't budge.

"Is there anything I just said you didn't understand?" Davis asked.

They both shook their heads.

"Anything I said that needs repeating?" He didn't wait for them to respond. "Then good day. See yourselves out."

*Albertson.*

He was in with Hall, which was how he'd kept his job in this district. Monte had no doubt that Albertson had gone to Hall with all this bullshit. Monte clenched his fists as his temper flared. Tempted to go directly to Albertson and rip him a new one, Monte held back. At least until he calmed down.

**

At the end of the day, Monte placed the phone down on his desk. He had just gotten the call he had been anticipating and dreading at the same time.

*The call.*

It was months in the making. He'd done all he could do. Now, an offer had been made.

*How am I going to tell Jasmine?*

He wasn't comfortable thinking about it. He had no idea how to present it to her. She could either be deliriously happy or in a rage.

*Should I have kept her more informed along the way?*

No, that was not his style. He preferred not to speak about a work-in-progress. She might not see it that way, though. He ran the risk of her thinking he had been deceiving her all along. In one way, he wished he hadn't gotten the call at all. It would be so much easier.

Jasmine was smart, successful, determined, and focused. She had a plan formulated. The events since they'd reconnected made the timing even worse. Now, she might question everything he had said to her. She might doubt his sincerity. Worst of all, he could risk losing her.

His fists clenched and his heart palpitated. No, losing Jasmine wasn't an option. He wiped his hands along his pants and took a deep breath.

*How is she going to take the news?*

After work, he went home and changed. He didn't want to stall any longer, so lingering at home wouldn't be helpful. He headed out to the car and took a few deep breaths.

Monte pulled his vehicle up to her house. He parked across the street and sat there contemplating. As much as he dreaded conflict, it had to be done. Hell, Jasmine deserved better than this. He should have let her know from the beginning, but the wheels had started turning before he'd seen her again. He liked to keep the conversation focused on her, so it had never come up.

The night air chilled him as he approached her door and rang her bell.

"Who is it?" the voice asked beyond the door.

She was smart. She didn't open her door to just anyone like some folks did.

"Monte."

The lock clicked and the door swung open. Jasmine had a look of pleasant surprise on her face. How long would it remain?

"Hey, come on in." Jasmine pulled the door wide open and stepped aside.

He should have brought something over, but he didn't want to sugarcoat it.

"Can I get you a drink?"

Monte hesitated. "Yeah, that would be great. Thanks."

Jasmine's face registered something. He wasn't sure what, but his lackluster answer probably gave her a clue. She indicated for him to have a seat in the living room.

Monte had a seat and sighed. He removed his jacket and draped it over the edge of the chair. That deliberately placed distance between them, so he moved to the couch.

Jasmine returned, drinks in hand.

"One vodka gimlet, sir." She held a glass of red wine for herself. After she had a seat, Monte couldn't help but notice the look on her face that read something like, *Okay, why the heck are you here?*

"How was your day?" Monte asked.

"Terrific. How was yours?"

"Eventful."

"How so?"

"I got a phone call today. I have had something in the works for quite some time. For months." Monte took a sip of his gimlet. It was good. She could mix a drink. "I took a trip to Lafayette…"

"I remember."

"It was the final meeting in a series of meetings."

Monte went silent for a moment.

Jasmine spoke up. "I'm not a mind reader."

"I was offered a job. Director of School Performance for a small independent school district. The location's in southwest Louisiana."

Jasmine's expression froze.

Monte continued. "It's a long distance away."

"Not commutable," Jasmine quipped.

"No." Monte shook his head. "I would have to relocate."

"What's a Director of School Performance?"

"Someone who supervises the principals and then reports back to the superintendent. They want someone out-of-district so there are no prior relationships. No bias."

Jasmine nodded and stood up. "Good luck. I'm sure you'll be a wonderful....Director of School Performance. Now, if you'll excuse me, I was working on my portfolio, and I need to get back to it. You can see yourself out."

Jasmine left the room.

Monte wanted to follow her but it wasn't the right time. She had to digest the information before he could discuss it with her further. He didn't want to leave her, but he couldn't say anything more at this point. Hopefully, she'd listen to what he had to say when the time was right.

*Will she?*

He had to give her at least a day. After he placed his unfinished drink on the table, he quietly let himself out.

\*\*

Jasmine tried to pull the dagger out of her heart, but she couldn't find the handle. It took her a moment to realize there was no handle. The blade was stuck in there. The seduction. The invitation to drinks and a candlelit dinner. All for nothing.

*Bastard. He's been job-hunting for months. Why the hell didn't he tell me?*

The hollowness inside her hurt. Her temples throbbed

and she wanted to break something. Possibly his neck.

*This is how men complicate things.*

To hell with him. She had a career to pursue. And hopefully, as far away from Monte as possible.

"Bastard," she muttered even though there was no one to hear her.

"Bastard!"

She'd seen Lynda Day George scream that out in some cheapo horror movie on cable and always wanted to say it herself. Jasmine refilled her wineglass and held it up to the light.

"Here's to you, Lynda Day George."

Jasmine laughed. It only took a moment for the laughter to turn into tears, and in her rage, she managed to avoid sobbing. Too angry to sob, she dabbed her eyes with a paper towel.

She dropped her wineglass into the sink, shattering it. Oddly, the noise it made calmed her.

*How can I be so stupid?*

Lose focus due to a man. Get kicked to the curb. The gut instinct had been right—stay focused on the career, let everything else go. But she hadn't let him go. When she'd seen him again, she'd known she couldn't resist him. She should have. Pushed him away. Told him no. Something. Anything. And now, look what had happened.

Lesson learned. Her master's degree had to be her sole goal now. No distractions. No excuses.

*Fool.*

Nothing good ever came from a one-night stand. She

should have been smart enough to see that. Maybe they'd both wanted the same thing. Revive the passion they'd shared for one night.

And move on.

Only they hadn't moved on. Monte had wanted more, and she'd fallen for him. After he'd gotten what he wanted, he'd seized the next opportunity. And here she stood, wounded and the world's biggest idiot for trusting him.

# CHAPTER NINETEEN

The next day—her last—Jasmine stepped out of her car in front of Brookhaven, her heart in her stomach. After taking a deep breath, she clutched her handbag and took the first step. She dreaded walking through those red doors, but she was here for her students. It had been painful to get out of bed and face the day. At least their faces would boost her spirits.

She signed in, averting her gaze from the direction of *his* office, and sprinted upstairs to her classroom. Vacant and silent, the room reminded her that she'd allowed him to touch her here.

Jasmine returned to her preparations. She didn't have much planned. Being the day before the holiday break, she'd anticipated the boys' energy levels would be high and concentration low.

When her class arrived, she tried to put on a front for her boys, but they could see right through her.

"What's the matter, Mizz Landers?"

"Come on, you can tell us."

"You just sad 'cause you won't see us again."

It was Tuesday, the day of their performance. Jasmine needed to get through this day, somehow, without ever making contact with one Monte Davis. She'd already received a new assignment from Mr. Whitney beginning on Monday. Seeing her kids perform tonight would be the last time she'd see them, and she hoped they'd understand.

"You lookin' forward to tonight?"

Jasmine managed a smile. "Sure, Corey."

The tall boy gave her a hug, and Jasmine fought back tears. The hug was exactly what she needed.

"We gonna practice some more?"

"It's not necessary. I don't think it's a good idea to practice the day of a performance. We want it to be fresh. You guys did great yesterday, and I am sure you'll be great tonight."

Dennis approached her. "I hope my mama comes tonight so you can meet her."

"I'd like that, Dennis." Wow. A student who actually wanted his mother to meet the teacher? Had she gotten to them that intimately so quickly? Would all her classes be a blessing like this one?

She should invite Louise. It might be *fuuuuuun*. They were supposed to meet up later anyway, and Louise had been curious about Brookhaven. Jasmine made a mental note to send her a text on her break.

"Do we have homework over Thanksgiving break?" LeRoy asked.

"No. Would you like some?"

"No!" eleven voices shouted back.

Jasmine laughed, thrilled she'd reached this point with them. Their sensitivity meant a lot to her, and she hoped she'd made a difference in their young lives. No lessons for today. The boys did their own independent activities. She didn't have the energy to be herself. Besides, she wanted to give them a "light day," as Demetrius would call it.

She slipped out of Brookhaven as quickly as possible at the end of the day. Sad to leave, yet at the same time, she didn't want a lot of long goodbyes. There were other schools and opportunities ahead of her. It would take a lot of work to get there, but she could do it.

Jasmine plopped down on her bed as soon as she got through the door. The performance was at six o'clock, which allowed plenty of time for a nap. Louise had sent a text back, and they planned to drive over together. That way, Jasmine wouldn't be alone and vulnerable to a Monte encounter.

Under the covers of her bed, she tried to forget Monte. She couldn't. When she closed her eyes, she imagined his strong, muscular body on hers, her heat aching for his massive cock. Her body shivered, for Monte brought her more in touch with her sexuality than any man. With him, she'd never become more of a woman.

*That's over.*

When she woke from her nap, she fixed a snack. She'd be having dinner with Louise later, so nothing heavy…just a few slices of green apple and some Jarlsberg cheese. Her hand trembled, and she feared how she might respond if she ran into Monte tonight.

*What to wear?*

Not the same thing she wore to school today. That would be so tacky. She had gone home, so she certainly planned on changing into something different. After popping the last slice of apple into her mouth, she headed upstairs to peruse her closet.

Jasmine stood in her walk-in, trying to decide what her Brookhaven swan-song outfit should be. Most of the staff would be there. Possibly many of her students' parents. Jasmine wanted to look presentable for her students and their parents but didn't want to attract any unnecessary attention from Monte.

Her body quivered as she pushed hanger after hanger aside, trying to find the right look for tonight.

*Drab? Chic? Old school? Sunday best? Jeans and a T-shirt? The nines? Cocktail outfit? Potato sack?*

She grabbed a garment bag and pulled out a hanger still wrapped in clear plastic from the dry cleaners.

"I'll go out the way I came in," Jasmine said.

She hung up the garment on a hook behind her closet door and then headed to the bathroom to take a quick shower. Glancing at the clock, she noticed it was only four forty-five. She still had plenty of time.

Later, she buckled her seatbelt in the passenger seat of Louise's car as Louise backed out of Jasmine's driveway and hit the road.

"How's lover boy?"

"I don't know who you're talking about," Jasmine said. She wasn't in the mood to discuss Monte with anyone. Her heart still heavy, she'd rather forget about him at the moment. Difficult since they were headed over to Brookhaven. It was a cool evening, but Jasmine had rolled down the window a bit and allowed the cool air to snap her to her senses.

"So I get to see these little rays of sunshine of yours?"

Jasmine gave her a sharp glance.

"The students, I mean."

"Yes, but I'm afraid you may have to sit through a bunch of crap before that. I'm not sure what the other teachers put together."

Jasmine wasn't even sure of the order of the program. Miss Johnson and one of the other teachers had organized it. Jasmine paused. "Did that make me sound conceited?"

Louise nodded. "Yes. You look nice. Forgot to say something earlier."

"Thank you. It's the same suit I wore my first day."

"Chanel to an elementary school? Fancy."

Monte dressed as sharp as a tack, but those under him didn't follow his example. Dana looked impeccably well groomed for her age, but even she wore loose-fitting clothing that seemed to hang on her. Poor Miss B in the office appeared to wear the same thing every day, except her hair was always done up with different bows and combs to distract from her outfit.

*Why am I thinking about that?*

As they pulled into the parking lot, the first floor of Brookhaven was lit up, while the second floor remained dark. BROOKHAVEN GIVES THANKS read the big sign posted by the main entrance. Miss Johnson greeted them at the door.

"Welcome, Miss Landers," she said and then turned to Louise and took her hand. "I'm Clarice Johnson. Welcome to Brookhaven."

"Louise Bennett. Nice to meet you."

"You look nice, Miss Johnson," Jasmine told her. Miss Johnson wore an ivory dress and a sparkling brooch. A fancy hat sat on her head, and her earrings matched her brooch. She handed them both programs.

Once inside, they found seats. Not many parents had arrived yet, but there had been a steady stream of cars pulling into the lot behind them.

Jasmine spotted Dana sitting in the front row. Her hair, usually worn straight, stood piled on top of her head with ringlets down the sides and a decorative pin. Her makeup, usually a simple base with a soft lipstick, was now accented with rouge streaks and darker shades.

*Her evening look.*

And the gentleman next to her, dressed to the nines, Jasmine didn't recognize. Did Dana have a date? The man, older than Dana, seemed to hang on her every word as she chattered away.

Dana caught Jasmine staring at her and waved. Jasmine smiled, the broadest grin she could muster, and waved back. She could have sworn Dana blushed before turning back to her date.

The auditorium burst with decorations of brown and yellow. The large BROOKHAVEN sign appeared on the back wall of the stage. Soft music filtered through the old speakers on either side of the stage. Jasmine glanced through the program and groaned. Her boys were second-to-last just before the special education class.

*Sure, put the repeaters near the back of the bus.*

"We're in for a treat," Jasmine said, the sarcasm dripping from her voice.

Louise looked at her and Jasmine pointed to the program. "This is my class."

Dana's program was up first. It promised to be a display of what the trees, the plants, the land, etc., must have looked like in 1621. Then again, Dana taught second grade. Maybe that was all the little tykes were capable of doing. The fifth grade class did a reenactment of what the first Thanksgiving might have been like. It was more comical than reverent.

Jasmine glanced around the auditorium and spotted Monte standing in the back. She quickly looked away before he had a chance to make eye contact. Her heart palpitated and her head went dizzy for a moment.

"This is kinda cute," Louise said.

"Kinda cute," Jasmine murmured. She closed her eyes and hoped her heart rate would return to normal. She's known he'd be here tonight. No way of avoiding him. But she had to be here for her kids. They'd become so attached to her, and she to them. She couldn't let them down by staying away over a man.

Louise turned around. "There he is."

"I saw him. Now, turn around and watch the, um, entertainment."

"So he's blowing town over a fatter paycheck?"

Jasmine nodded. "I guess. Or the prestige of the position. Even though I have no idea what the heck his new title means."

"Which is what?"

"Director of School Personnel or something like that. Performance, not personnel."

"Sounds like one of those jobs they give in public education just to fill up their budget."

Jasmine's gaze focused straight ahead. She could not care less if Monte stood behind them, even though her body indicated otherwise. Jasmine suffered through a few more skits, but she noticed that Louise seemed to be amused. Good for her. Finally, her boys were up. The music blasted loudly, which was exactly what Jasmine wanted. The hip-hop song would wake up this audience. Her boys bounded onto the stage and performed brilliantly. They had energy, enthusiasm, and exuded charisma. Jasmine did not expect anything less.

After the dance ended, the applause thundered through the auditorium. When it died down, Tyrone held up a card with a large letter T on it. The cards had been laid out at the foot of the stage, but she hadn't noticed them before Tyrone picked one up. Jasmine had no idea what was going on—they hadn't rehearsed that with her.

All the boys at once shouted, "Tolerant."

Tyrone said, "Miss Landers is tolerant of all of our crazy selves."

Jasmine sank into her chair.

*What is this?*

DaShon held up an H.

All the boys shouted, "Helpful."

DaShon said, "Miss Landers always gives us the help we need."

Louise turned to Jasmine and beamed.

LeRoy held up an A.

All the boys shouted, "Advice."

LeRoy said, "Miss Landers always gives good advice."

Lazarus held up an N.

The boys shouted, "Nice."

Lazarus said "Miss Landers is nice to us and does not treat us like kids."

Jasmine had sunk so low in her chair she was certain she was going to fall to the floor. She had no idea the boys thought so highly of her. She gazed at them, her heart warmed. If there was any doubt in her mind about her new career direction, this was the confirmation. She'd reached those boys in a way she hadn't imagined.

Could she have reached so deeply in such a short time? She wasn't even a certified teacher. Maybe they needed someone who would listen to them as individuals. That, Jasmine did.

Dennis held up a K.

The boys shouted, "Kind."

Dennis said, "Miss Landers is always kind to us."

Louise squeezed Jasmine's hand.

Demetrius held up an S.

The boys shouted, "Sincere!"

Demetrius said, "Miss Landers tells us what she really means."

Corey held up a G.

The boys shouted, "Giving!"

Corey said, "Miss Landers has given us so much of herself."

**

In the back of the auditorium, Monte's gaze was transfixed on the stage. He could not believe these were the same boys he had known for years. Some of them a full seven years from pre-K, kindergarten, first through third grade, and fourth grade twice. Something welled up inside him. Something he had not experienced in a very long time.

Pierre held up an I.

The boy shouted, "Instruction!"

Pierre said, "Miss Landers is a good teacher."

Monte tried to swallow the lump in his throat.

Jordan held up a V.

The boys shouted, "Vacant."

Jordan said, "That's what our hearts will feel with Miss Landers gone."

That did it. Monte could not hold back any longer. His body quivered and moisture welled in his eyes. The tears started streaming down his face.

Terrance held up an I.

The boys shouted, "Ideal."

Terrance said, "Miss Landers is the ideal person."

Monte's tears made his whole body shake. He placed his

hand over his mouth so as not to call attention to himself.

Jamal held up an N.

The boys shouted, "Neighbor!"

Jamal said, "Miss Landers is one of us now!"

Jamal was the last of the boys, but there was one letter left, so he placed the N down and held up a G.

The boys shouted, "God!"

Jamal said, "That's who sent Miss Landers to us."

Monte ran from the auditorium and dashed to his car. He collapsed into a bundle of hard, heavy sobs. For the first time since his wife's passing, he cried. The boys' love for Jasmine made it clear what he'd been fighting all along: his own love for her. He'd allowed sex to mask his true feelings, but tonight, he had no doubt that he loved Jasmine.

His body shook and chest heaved. He pressed his palms against his thighs and tried to regulate his breathing. When he became light-headed, he lowered his head. Fear stabbed through him and he closed his eyes.

Years of suppressed emotion. Months of denial. Finally, acceptance. Ellie had been laid to rest and was gone for good, and it was time to move on. His shoulders heaved up and down, no longer heavy with the burden he'd carried. A few deep breaths.

Why hadn't he seen it sooner? How could he have been in denial for so long? The day Jasmine stepped into his school as a substitute teacher he had known it. Yet he'd hidden. Pretended it wasn't happening. Lied to himself. But not anymore.

*I'm in love with Jasmine.*

# CHAPTER TWENTY

Monte stretched across his bed, his head pounding with a nasty headache.

*They love her. Those boys really love her.*

How could he be stupid and greedy for a raise and a better position? He didn't need the money. He had plenty of it. The only thing on his mind at the time had been boosting his retirement income. That was a single-minded, silly mistake. Jumping at an opportunity without seeing the bigger picture.

Jasmine Landers excited him. Fiercely independent, successful, self-made, and compassionate, she had so many qualities he admired. The courage she took to pursue a noble career, the connections she'd made with her students, all added up to one special lady.

*I love her. I really love her.*

Had it really taken the words of eleven young men to make him realize that? No, he'd known he loved her for a while, he just hadn't known how to admit it to himself. He was crippled by the grief from his wife's passing, and he needed time to sort out his feelings.

He rolled over and punched the pillow. Here he was a grown, successful man in his mid-thirties, and he couldn't express himself to a woman. He had messed up big-time and he needed to right a wrong. Two years of masking his feelings had resulted in nothing but loneliness. Now, he could lose the woman he loved if he didn't act.

Monte rolled out of bed and headed for the bathroom. He found some ibuprofen in the medicine cabinet and popped a couple into his mouth. He swallowed the pills with some water, hoping this would quell his headache.

*What can I say to her now?*

The truth. Admit how a foolish decision blinded rational thinking. How blind ambition masked what the heart wanted. He'd spent nearly a year reliving that night, and when she'd walked into his life again, he'd struggled. How could he have been so smooth with her that night in New Orleans and so awkward here in Portsmith?

Of course it was awkward. She worked at his school. He hadn't really owned the grieving process or his lack of acceptance. Could he imagine that a new job in a new town, letting go of this house and all its memories, would somehow make things right?

But that would be running. And running never resolved anything. He'd stay here, embrace the job he had now, and commit to the woman he loved.

*Jasmine.*

He had to make things right between them. Make her understand. Find a sincere way to get through to her.

Apologize for being an asshole by accepting that job. Or rather, for keeping the whole process so secretive.

If he didn't move and lay still on the bed, his head wouldn't hurt as much. The headache had to pass before he could do anything. Monte closed his eyes and remained as motionless as possible.

*I have to go to her.*

Once he could move again, once the migraine passed, he had to see her. It was imperative to make her understand how wrong he'd been. He'd been foolishly seduced by a carrot dangled in front of him, and he'd been wrong to take the bait.

He didn't need the job. He needed Jasmine. She meant so much more to him than a cursory job decision. All his career goals in education had been achieved. His personal hopes and dreams, shattered. If only she could have seen the change in him tonight, unleashed by those eleven boys and the love they'd expressed.

*It's not too late.*

# CHAPTER TWENTY-ONE

The day before Thanksgiving, Jasmine sipped a cup of coffee and waited for Martha. Jasmine had given her housekeeper the rest of the holiday week off, so she needed her today. Once this long weekend had ended, Jasmine could get back to her career and put the hurt of Monte behind her.

Jasmine had dinner plans at her aunt's house tomorrow, a family tradition for years, but she really needed to get her own house in good shape. Inevitably, someone always dropped in, sniffing around for a cocktail during the holiday weekend.

"I appreciate your being here," Jasmine said. "I know you must have plenty to do at your house."

"Just cook for Anthony. But you know how it is at my house. All kinds of folks just show up even if they didn't get an invitation."

"I don't know how you do it."

"They know they're gonna get a plate of food at my place." Martha chuckled.

"You're a good cook. You can't blame them."

"Oh, I'm all right, I suppose."

Jasmine completed her formal application to Southeastern and saved it until she had her test scores. As a Plan B, she decided to apply to Florida as well. With the mood she was in, the change of scenery might suit her well. She knocked out that application as well and took pride in that task accomplished. Now all she needed to do was study her test prep materials and schedule those tests.

Her cell phone rang with a call from Monte. Her finger hit the reject button and sent that sucker to voicemail. There was nothing he could say to her now.

"Did you want some tea?" Martha asked.

"No, thanks. I filled up on coffee."

Jasmine liked the way Martha made herself at home here. In some ways, Jasmine figured Martha took better care of her house because of it.

She stepped outside into the chilly November day to check the birdfeeders. The sun was bright and the air fresh, and she retrieved the birdseed and filled them up. Jasmine loved seeing birds in her backyard. She also had a bright blue birdbath for them, kept full from rainwater.

The morning was still young, and shopping still had to be done. So much to do around the holiday, and it was only one day.

Later that morning, Jasmine strolled around the mall looking for a hostess gift for her aunt. Her mind was elsewhere, though, trying to put into perspective the events of the past week. The pain and the disappointment were hard to shake. She had trusted Monte, had given herself to him—and even loved him.

*I still do.*

Was it selfish to not be happy for him? Monte was successful, ambitious, and focused. He'd led a career-driven life. To get an opportunity like the one he'd been offered was cause for celebration.

*I reacted all wrong.*

Prestige and position were important to Monte. Hadn't he spent fifteen years working to better himself? He deserved to move up the ladder.

She couldn't focus on the task at hand and asked the saleswoman for some help.

"Excuse me, do you have anything new and interesting? I want to bring my aunt a hostess gift tomorrow."

"Sure, come around here and let me show you a few things," the elderly woman said. The shop was stacked with unique and pretty items. Her aunt liked anything for the kitchen, and there were plenty of interesting items to choose from.

Jasmine settled on a pretty set of espresso cups and saucers. She had the store gift- wrap it for her. As she waited for the wrapping, she made her decision.

*Of course I can go.*

With four more days off, Jasmine began to formulate a plan. She could even call Whitney and cancel next week's assignment if need be. She could leave tomorrow after dinner. Jasmine pulled her cell phone from her purse. Scrolling through her numbers, she found the one she needed.

"Yvonne, it's Jasmine. Yes! I know, right?... I'm doing

great. How are you?" Jasmine paused to listen but was in a hurry. "Listen, how would you like some company over the long weekend?"

\*\*

Monte debated whether he should go to Jasmine now or if he should give her more time. He needed to see her and to speak with her, but he wouldn't be surprised if she wasn't ready to speak to him. But nothing would stop him. He had every intention of winning her back. He had to. Without Jasmine, he had no chance for happiness again.

He'd spent the day preparing for tomorrow's holiday, a simple dinner with Wendell and a few wayward colleagues who had nowhere else to go. He'd invited Jasmine to join him, but she had a standing invite at her aunt's. Understandable. Family came first.

Holidays were a time for family if one had any. He had his nephew, Wendell. Jasmine had her aunt. Something to be thankful for at this time of the year.

He had been so wrapped up in the passion of their romance that he had not seen the big picture.

*I messed up.*

He had all the food he needed, bought it well in advance. No fighting through long lines in a grocery store the day before Thanksgiving. All he needed to do now was check the wine pairings, as he might need to make a liquor store run.

*She didn't take my call.*

No reason why she should. He had knocked her between the eyes with his announcement about the job. What an idiot he'd been. Now, he had to wait until she was ready to listen. Jasmine probably didn't want to hear another word from him at this point, but he had more he needed to tell her.

*I'm crazy.*

He shouldn't, but he did it anyway. He couldn't wait any longer. He drove over to Jasmine's house unannounced. He would use the pretense that he was dropping off a bottle of holiday cheer. Of course, she would see right through him.

Monte pulled up to her driveway. Her car wasn't there.

*If I leave it at the door, will she know it's from me?*

Monte walked up the drive to the house and was certain of some movement by a window. That was odd. He took a chance and knocked on the door. In a moment, the door swung open.

"May I help you?"

It was a gray-haired woman with steely-blue eyes. Jasmine had mentioned she had an aunt. Or was this the housekeeper?

"Hi, I'm Monte Davis. Is Miss Landers at home?"

"No, sir, she just left."

"Oh, would you kindly give her this bottle of wine?"

He handed it to the woman, and she accepted it.

"Yes, sir."

"Thank you," Monte said, gave her a short wave, and retreated to his car.

*Strike two.*

Monte had an uphill battle on his hands. He finished a few errands and then went back home to prepare the table for tomorrow. Tablecloth, good china, and decorations all had to be brought down from an upstairs storage room. He had help as well, but he seldom burdened his maid. He liked to do things for himself. It kept his mind occupied and off matters of the heart. Jasmine wasn't answering her phone and wasn't home.

*What can I try next?*

His maid had picked up the centerpiece for him, since he had no clue what to get, but he did the rest. Monte nodded, admiring his table setting.

*There's not going to be a strike three.*

# CHAPTER TWENTY-TWO

Thanksgiving dinner at Aunt Harriet's brought back memories of Jasmine's childhood. She and her parents had come to this house every year for the holiday. Continuing the tradition at her aunt's helped her feel connected to her parents, long gone.

Back then, a kids' table had been set up in the kitchen. The small children, like Jasmine, sat there with distant cousins she didn't really know. As they were served plates of carved turkey, two kinds of potatoes, gravy, and cranberry sauce, they'd chatter about each other's toys or the television shows they favored. The cousins had traveled from someplace out of state once a year on Thanksgiving, but otherwise she couldn't recall having seen them any other time. Eventually, they'd lost touch.

Harriet, known for her decorating skills, went all out. Every room in the house featured Thanksgiving crafts.

"Everything looks so beautiful, Aunt Harriet. As always."

"Thank you. You know how much I love this holiday."

"Your favorite."

"You got that right."

Jasmine handed her a shopping bag. "For you."

Harriet unwrapped the gift and opened the box. "Oh, they're bea-u-ti-ful," she said with her southern drawl.

"I forgot to buy the machine to go with it."

"You know, I think there's one in the garage." Harriet gazed at the cups. "Thank you, Jasmine."

"Thank you for having me."

Harriet had everything prepared for dinner. Jasmine's attempts to help her in the kitchen were futile. There wasn't anything left to do except eat.

After dinner, right on schedule, Jasmine got into her Lexus and hit the freeway. Her packed bag was in the trunk. As planned, she would stop at a motel along the way and continue the drive in the morning.

Jasmine had hit the road when the sun was still up, but barely. It would be dark soon, but the route was familiar. She'd traveled it before when she went to visit some of her old college friends. It had been a long time, though, and Jasmine didn't want to spend too much of her time driving at night.

She stopped in Greendale to get some sleep at the Archer Country Inn. It was clean and comfortable, which was all that mattered. Unfortunately, sleep did not come easily. Monte kept creeping into her mind.

In the morning, after a quick breakfast, Jasmine resumed her drive.

She arrived in Florida by noon Friday, thrilled when she finally pulled up to Yvonne's condo and rang the bell.

"Jazzie!!!" Yvonne shouted when she opened the door. Jazzie was a nickname Jasmine was given in college but was one she'd like to forget. She certainly didn't let anyone in Portsmith call her that.

Jasmine threw her arms around her friend and gave her a big hug. Yvonne was a tall young woman, Jasmine's age, with a beautiful head of thick hair. Yvonne's eyes were a sparkling green set among her clear, caramel complexion.

Inside, Jasmine was seated on the couch as Yvonne prepared a snack in the kitchen.

"I want to hear all about him," Yvonne yelled from the galley.

"Who?"

"Whoever you're seeing these days."

"I'm not," Jasmine answered flatly. She didn't want to talk about him. Didn't even want to think about him. This weekend promised to be about her and her friends. Nothing more.

Yvonne came into the living room with a tray of bread, cheese, and tea.

"Then to what do I owe the honor of *this* visit?"

Jasmine's face flushed. The last time she came to visit Yvonne, it was after a bad breakup with a man. It wasn't Jasmine's intention to repeat that.

"I'm going back to college to get my master's degree. Florida is one of the colleges I'm considering."

"Why not?" Yvonne said as she poured the tea. "It worked for your undergraduate degree. Hey, it would be awesome to have you here again."

"It would be awesome to be here," Jasmine agreed. "I still

need to make up my mind, though. I didn't know anyone in the graduate-studies department when I was here, so I want to meet some people."

"I know some people. Graduate studies in what?" Yvonne poured more coffee. She'd bee a student at the university the same time Jasmine attended. Now, Yvonne worked in the dean's office and had a side business doing hair out of her house on the weekends.

"Education."

"Oh, sure. I know the department chair. Nice lady named Carmen."

"I'd appreciate it if you could introduce me."

"On a holiday weekend?"

Jasmine laughed. "No, on Monday morning. The point of coming down now was to spend time with you. It's great to see you, Yvonne."

"Evie. Don't be so formal, girl." Yvonne swallowed a bite of cheese. "So what do you want to do until Monday?"

"Everything. Keep busy. Have fun. See the old sights. I just want to take my mind off of everything in Portsmith."

"Oh." Yvonne grinned. "So there *was* a man."

Jasmine shook her head. "We're not going to talk about that now. We have too much catching up to do. What's going on with you?"

Yvonne shrugged her shoulders. "Not a lot new. Work is going great! I love what I do. The university's a fun place to work. Then, as far as the hair business goes, I've built up an awesome client base. Derrick is still my on-again, off-again. Life is good."

"Oh, you'll have appointments this weekend."

"Well, because of the holiday, no. I was booked like crazy last week. So anything you want to do, we'll do it." Yvonne grinned. "Within reason."

Jasmine giggled and picked up a wedge of cheese. "Where did you get this?"

"I picked it up at that little place on Mayberry and Ninth."

"It's still there?"

"Yes, it's a relief some of the mom-and-pop stores are still here. I should have gotten some wine."

"We can always get that when we hit the club tonight."

"The club? Jazzie, you are in a mood!"

Jasmine smirked and helped herself to another wedge of cheese. She was determined to make this a trip she would not forget. Fun. Pure, unadulterated fun. That was the plan for this weekend.

But she couldn't quell Monte's effect on her. She'd lost a man she'd never had. Her heart sank, and her stomach had that empty feeling. So much emptiness. How could she'd fill it?

*By focusing on my career, that's how. And not on Monte.*

# CHAPTER TWENTY-THREE

Monte looked out the window, his heart heavy. The drizzle had turned into a heavy rain. Black Friday, the day after Thanksgiving, and Monte had decided to spend it at home. The last thing he would do today was step foot in a retail store. He watched the morning news, featuring footage of people being trampled when the doors opened at five in the morning. It was sad to see society reduced to that.

A wave of hopelessness had overcome him since he'd woken. Not that he'd slept much last night. So much unsaid weighed on his mind, and he still couldn't make contact with Jasmine. The pain intensified with each passing hour.

Wendell had spent the night and was still asleep. That guy could sleep all day and probably would do just that.

As the rain pelted against the windows, Monte tried to come up with a way to communicate with Jasmine. How could he express how wrong he'd been not to keep her informed? He should have been transparent from the day she'd stepped into Brookhaven.

His body sank into the chair, somber, and his heart like

lead in his chest. So much time to ponder and so much he'd like to express.

*I have to see her and let her know.*

He had driven by her house late yesterday afternoon with a plate of food, but her car was gone. She continued to ignore his calls. In fact, Monte suspected she had turned her phone off. He wished he could remember the name of her friend whom Miss Johnson had met Tuesday night. Unfortunately, his mind drew a blank.

*Maybe she just needs more time.*

He wasn't patient. Monte closed the drapes and lit the fireplace. The fire engulfed the logs, and the room glowed from the light of the flames.

When he sat in the chair, his hands clutched the fabric on the arms. The realization struck him that he'd messed up big time. After two years, he'd finally found a woman he could love. Sadly, he'd found that out too late.

*Jasmine's got a new assignment beginning Monday.*

Perhaps he could find out where. Calvin Whitney was under no obligation to tell him, but Monte suspected he would. Hopefully, he wouldn't have to, as he wanted to see Jasmine before Monday. He wished he hadn't let this much time pass. He should have righted his wrong as soon as possible.

*Damn.*

What could she be thinking? And where was she? He hadn't been able to contact her at home in days.

The house stood so lonely. Even with Wendell here, the emptiness was overwhelming. Wendell spent most of his time sleeping and eating. He could pack away calories and he was in great shape. Monte had no idea how Wendell burned it off.

*There's too much of Ellie in this house.*

It remained a shrine rather than the memory it should be. He'd have to make some changes here, even before he put it up for sale. Perhaps when Wendell woke, he could help out. Two years and nothing had changed.

Some of the furniture had to go. The pictures were too many. Most could be stored away and one left remaining. He'd donated all her clothes, at the insistence of a friend. But aside from that, he'd left too much the same for two years.

He put his head in his hands and squeezed his eyes shut. It had been foolish to hang on to his grief for so long. Opportunities denied. Chances not taken. His body shook and he breathed deeply.

*Time to move on.*

"What's up?"

Monte's head snapped to the side. "I didn't hear you coming."

"I just woke up." Wendell yawned.

He certainly looked like he just woke. If anything, he'd overslept. The clothes he'd slept in were rumpled, his hair was specked with lint, and his eyelids were half-mast.

"Help yourself to some coffee. The decanter's filled with a fresh pot."

Wendell sat down and poured some into a mug.

"What are you doing?" Wendell asked.

"Nothing," Monte said. "Enjoying the peace and quiet."

"Well, I'm up. That's over." Wendell grinned.

Monte might as well tell Wendell what was on his mind. It had been a good holiday, and Wendell's spirits seemed high this weekend.

"How did you sleep?"

"Great." Wendell downed another swig of coffee.

"Wendell, I think it might be time for me to move on."

"Move on?"

"Sell the house. Let go. Move forward."

"Why would you sell this?" Wendell's face crumbled with alarm. He'd hang out here most weekends and considered it a safe haven. Monte had to reassure him he wasn't taking that away from him.

Monte sighed. "It's not easy. Losing a wife. A partner. Coming home every day to the home we shared. It's not easy at all."

Wendell nodded. "It's that woman."

"What do you mean?"

"That woman at your school. You love her."

Monte met Wendell's gaze. Could Wendell have seen it all along? Was it apparent that day in the Blooming Cactus? "Yes, I do."

"Have you told her?"

"No, not yet."

"Will you?"

"Yes. How do you feel about it?"

Wendell shrugged. "How do *you* feel about it?"

"Good. I haven't felt this way since…"

"Yeah, I know."

"I want to know you're okay with it."

Wendell stared into his coffee cup for a moment and then nodded.

"You sure?"

"I wouldn't say sure. But I do understand. You got needs."

"That's not what I'm taking about."

"I know, just messin' wit you."

"When I think about Jasmine, I think about my future."

Wendell nodded and lowered his eyes. "You deserve to be happy again."

"Are we good?"

"We're good."

"That's all I ask," Monte said. "I want things to be okay with everybody. I don't think that's a lot to ask for—it's fair."

"Life's not always fair."

"True."

"What next?"

"I'm not sure. I have to see her and talk to her before I can say what's next."

*But when?*

# CHAPTER TWENTY-FOUR

Monday morning, Monte breathed a sigh of relief. Mrs. Cage had returned to work and in good health. Brookhaven slowly got back into the daily grind. He missed having Jasmine here, but that might be a blessing. It would've been tough for them to have anything meaningful while both working here.

He ran a finger over the framed picture of his late wife, then removed it from his desktop and placed it in a drawer. It shouldn't have sat there for so long. Tears welled in his eyes as he pushed the drawer closed.

*Yes, it most certainly is time to move on.*

Later, Monte sat in his office on the phone with Calvin Whitney, perplexed.

*Jasmine cancelled her assignment.*

That was not like her at all. She loved what she did. Whitney said she had sounded fine on the phone, so at least Monte assumed she was safe. He just had no idea what was going on with her.

"I don't understand why she did it. I'm the one who was

stuck without a substitute at Hillsdale."

"Let me know if you hear anything further," Monte said and hung up the phone.

*Perhaps she's out of town.*

Over the weekend, Monte had driven by her home, but the driveway remained empty and the house dark. No sign of her at all. Not even posts on Facebook.

Nothing could stop him. He planned on seeing Jasmine again, speaking with her, and letting her know what was really going on with him. But it proved more difficult with each passing day.

His gut hurt thinking about the pain he'd caused her. But he'd make it right. If only she'd give him a chance. Too many chances had passed. He wasn't about to let her get away, at least not without expressing himself to her.

No time to hold back. He'd find her, and he hoped she'd listen. The days of being a repressed grieving widower were behind him.

She could be staying with her aunt, but Monte didn't know where the aunt lived, nor did he want to intrude. He recalled Jasmine had mentioned the name of her church. His only remaining hope of seeing her was to stop by the service on Wednesday evening.

*Still two days away.*

# CHAPTER TWENTY-FIVE

Jasmine woke Tuesday morning in the same Archer Country Inn along the freeway, anxious to get home. She had been too tired to continue driving last night, so she reluctantly stopped here again. It wasn't so bad. Cheap rooms. Shabby furniture. But at least it was clean. And warm.

Was this what a change in career would bring? When her fashion business was at its peak, she'd stay in four-star hotels. Her new career came with adjustments. Jasmine pulled the blankets around her and lay still for a moment, staring at the window. The red curtains with the morning sunshine behind them cast a warm glow over the room.

She had a bit of fruit and yogurt from the breakfast bar to tide her over before starting the last leg of her drive. From a television mounted on the wall, an anchor droned on about the weather. At least the forecast looked clear for her trip home.

Travel. Road trips were so exciting when embarking on the outbound journey. But driving back home was all about burning rubber. Although Jasmine didn't mind the driving.

*Alone.*

Endless miles of road with nothing to distract her gave her plenty of time to think. Career, career, career. That had been her credo all her life, and it wasn't about to change. The only thing that changed was the type of career.

Distractions proved dangerous. Giving in to them could lead down a path of disappointment. She wouldn't make that mistake again.

*Of course he took the job. I would have done the same.*

Was that so different from researching schools out of state? The roles could have been reversed. Showing up at his door one night and making a similar announcement.

*Hey, going to college in Florida. See ya.*

Monte had received a prestigious job offer and accepted the opportunity. Jasmine, in the same position, likely couldn't have turned it down. His career path had been different from hers: steady, by the book, rank-and-file steps up the educational ladder.

Jasmine had interned for a while in fashion, gotten a lowly job, and within a short time, struck out on her own. Freelance. Had built a business. Had been the boss for years.

There wasn't anywhere else for her to go in fashion. For Monte, it was different. In his career, it made sense to look for the next promotion. Like Yvonne, Monte had followed the straight and narrow path.

It had been awesome to see Yvonne again in Florida. She'd been ambitious Jasmine's undergraduate days. Now, she'd worked her way up to an associate dean. Photos of her career covered the walls of her office.

A pang of melancholy pierced Jasmine. What if she'd followed the same straight and narrow path that Yvonne had? Jasmine had been relentlessly independent, but to a fault. By insisting on doing everything in her own time and in her own way, she ended up burnt out by a cutthroat business. Yvonne, like Monte, had played it safe all those years.

But Jasmine celebrated Yvonne's success. She'd worked her way up from entry-level to a handsome position. Here Jasmine stood, at age thirty-two, starting over. Not from financial necessity, as Jasmine had plenty of money socked away. But from the desire to find fulfillment.

Maybe that's why she didn't see the big picture. Jasmine had spent her career as a free spirit, breaking away from tradition. Monte had followed tradition since day one and had never broken away.

*Plus, I like him. Denial isn't getting me anywhere.*

Her independence had basically been thrust on her when her parents passed at an early age. But she'd proven herself. Maybe it was time to be less stubborn. Switching to a new career, she'd have to be. She couldn't be so pigheaded working in public education.

The pursuit of a master's degree could lead to Florida. Was that any different? That would involve a big move. Leaving everything else behind. The house. The only family member she had left.

*Like Monte's doing for Lafayette.*

Besides, the weekend was more of a personal escape than a serious research trip. It had been too long since embarking on an adventure. Weekends like that were good for the soul.

*Monte.*

Desire and denial made for strange bedfellows. She couldn't resist his charms, his seduction. All he had to do was show up at her door, and he'd be in her bed.

Let him go off and plant his seed in Lafayette. But he'd better not be surprised if he got a visit from an old hookup. A weekend fling might be fun.

Right. It was so much more than that. She cared for him. They didn't know one another that well, but he'd been nothing but kind to her. Helpful with her career search, always volunteering information. He'd even tried to protect her from Albertson.

*And now I'm being selfish.*

Why not look for a job in Lafayette? Perhaps go to college in that area. Would that be so terrible? She had a house and an aunt in Portsmith, but that was about it. The fashion end of her business she could do anywhere. There wasn't any element of that based in Portsmith. What if she'd considered that earlier instead of only thinking of herself?

It was wrong to think of what she had with Monte as a one-night stand. She strongly suspected he believed that as well. Monte stood for something greater than a roll in the hay. A strong man, confident, and stable—what else could she ask for?

*Him, that's what.*

It was a bit before dark when she arrived home, and Jasmine headed straight for the bedroom. The empty bedroom. The one she shared with no one.

At thirty-two, maybe it was time to change that. She'd found a man she was crazy about.

She had no energy to do anything but discard her clothes and crawl under the covers. She sent a text to Louise as promised to say she'd returned. After she sent it, the phone slipped from her hand and landed on the floor. Now, sleep.

*I have to talk to him, but not tonight.*

When Jasmine woke the next morning, she didn't want to move from the comfort of her bed. Her body had needed to catch up on some of the sleep it missed over her partying weekend. She rolled over and closed her eyes, not ready to get up yet.

Eventually, she crawled out of bed and made it downstairs to the kitchen.

Jasmine prepared some dark-brewed coffee. Colleges, work, career, and a wounded heart. She had been somewhat successful at avoiding Monte while she was away. Here, in her kitchen, she couldn't stop thinking about him.

A piece of paper rested against a mug on the counter. It was a note from Martha informing her that there was plenty of food in the fridge and to please call her if she needed anything.

*What would I do without Martha?*

Jasmine picked up her phone and turned it on. It beeped like crazy to let her know the number of missed calls and missed texts. After a quick cup of coffee, she went right back to bed. Perhaps that was the kind of vacation she really had needed—nothing but bed rest.

Jasmine had no idea how many hours had passed when she woke, sluggish.

*Great. Now I got too much sleep.*

She crawled out of bed and made it back to the kitchen. The coffee from earlier in the day still sat in the carafe. After placing her hand on the glass and confirming it was cold, she poured a cup and placed it in the microwave. She still had the enormous chore of sorting through all her missed calls and texts, so she took care of that while sipping coffee.

*What an adventure.*

It had been a few years since she'd made that drive back and forth to Florida. Although the trip was brief, it had done her a world of good to see her friends again. Yvonne had been her best friend in college. Sure, they'd visited one another, but those days of hanging out and partying were long gone.

Maybe she could recapture some of that college spirit when she went back to get her master's. At least the prospect of going back to college excited her. Had it not been for her business taking off, she would have gone back years ago.

*Mmm.*

Even reheated, the coffee still satisfied her with rich flavor. She gazed at nothing, unfocused. Back home, now she had to focus on the future. On her new career.

That evening, she attended Wednesday evening service at her church, followed by a dinner. Seeing her church members again lifted her spirits. Familiar faces, many with a kind word to say. They were like an extended family.

"How was your holiday?" an elderly woman asked. She dressed in her usual finest, which often meant the same outfit she wore on Sunday.

"Lovely," Jasmine said. "Yours?"

"Oh, you know my grandbabies. They go all out for Thanksgiving and spoil me. Pastor Jackson joined us." She held her head back and thrust out her chest.

The pastor had probably visited a dozen families on Thanksgiving and made each one feel like they were the only family he'd graced with his presence.

"That's wonderful," Jasmine said. She moved away from the woman and joined the line.

Before she reached the table, she smelled the dinner. The aromas of chicken Parmesan with pasta, salad, and freshly baked bread filled the air. She hadn't the energy to cook tonight and was grateful for the Wednesday night suppers that followed the service.

"Nice to see you, Jasmine." Lenora smiled as she served Jasmine a heaping plate of salad. A regular member of the congregation, Lenora always had a kind word.

"You, too, Lenora. Did you have a nice holiday?"

"At my house, it's never anything but spectacular." She passed Jasmine's plate to the gentleman serving the main course.

With a full plate, Jasmine headed to a table to join some of her congregation. She didn't make it to service every Wednesday, but she tried. It often served as a welcome respite from the hectic responsibilities of running her fashion business.

"Good to see you," one of the ladies said to Jasmine as she sat.

"Thank you, you, too." Jasmine wasn't in a conversational

mood. The food smelled so good that all she wanted to do was eat.

The salad tasted fresh and had just the right amount of dressing. Vegetables always made her feel better. She needed to eat more of them. Portsmith had a reputation for fried food, which she almost always avoided. Maintaining a healthy diet in this town could be challenging.

Her day had been a haze of catching up on sleep and mircrowaved coffee. Before tonight, she hadn't eaten a thing all day. Music filtered through the room at a low tone, allowing members to converse with one another.

"May I join you?"

The sound of his voice reverberated through her, sending chills all over her body. She stared at her plate and didn't want to glance up, yet she did anyway.

*Monte.*

He stood before her, holding a plate, wearing a starched dress shirt and pressed trousers. She'd never seen him here before and had no idea why he'd come. Warmth rushed through her head and she tried to mask any hint of a reaction.

"Sure," she muttered, not wanting to attract the attention of others seated at the table.

Monte sat, and Jasmine turned her shoulder slightly away from him.

"Good evening. Monte Davis," he said to the people seated at the table.

When others chatted with him and introduced one another, it gave Jasmine a moment to compose herself.

*Why is he here?*

She hated the reaction her body had with him seated so close to her. Under the table, she used her napkin to wipe her sweaty palms. This was no random meeting. He had to know she'd be here, and he'd purposefully tracked her down.

"How have you been?" he asked.

"Fine," Jasmine said, staring down into her food, suddenly without an appetite.

"I've been worried about you."

"No need." Jasmine pushed the food around on her plate with a fork. The heat that stirred inside her betrayed her. She would wish him well on his way to Lafayette, and that would be that.

*No.*

She wanted him. That ache of desire didn't lie. With her gaze lowered, she fought the urge to turn to him. She feared that look of hunger he often displayed in his eyes. Along with pain. He wasn't ready for her and she didn't need him, so why did he play this game with her?

He'd have a nice life down in Lafayette Parish, and she'd forget all about him.

*Except I won't.*

Night after night, she dreamed of him making love to her. Dreamed about his touch. Desired him inside her again. Oh, if there was any man who could claim her, it was Monte.

But he had other priorities, as did she. Her career. Thanks to those boys, she had made a commitment and wouldn't back down. Back to college to get her master's, as she'd dreamed about for years. Now, it would soon be within her reach.

"I have something I need to tell you," Monte said.

"This is hardly the place." Jasmine spoke in a low tone. Her church members were a nosy group.

"Okay, it can wait until after we eat."

*After we eat? Is he kidding? This isn't a date.*

Some people in her congregation kept glancing at her, so she continued to eat, despite her lack of appetite. As much as she liked coming here, she wished the people weren't so into everyone else's personal business.

Monte chatted with some of the other folks at the table, which came as sort of a relief. She didn't want to be bothered with him. She had no idea why he was here and, frankly, couldn't imagine what he had to say to her. Goodbye wasn't necessary—she could do without that.

She'd struggled so much when she'd first seen him again. Did she or didn't she? Go for it or not? She'd gone for it, and look what had happened. All her hopes squashed.

The chicken was delicious. She really needed to get some nourishment in her. She'd done more driving than eating while she'd been away. Too bad tonight's dinner was ruined by an uninvited guest.

"Excuse me," Jasmine said to her tablemates.

She rose and put up her plate.

*How in the world did he know I was here?*

Monte followed her.

*He looks so handsome.*

"Is there someplace we can talk?" he asked.

*What does he want?*

She folded her arms, not sure how to respond. What he had to say to her didn't interest her in the slightest. But if she heard him out, maybe he'd go away.

"Yeah," she mumbled and turned on her heel.

The reading room was adjacent to the dining area yet far enough for privacy. A library of inspirational texts, it also served as a meeting room for small groups. Fortunately, the room was empty since the church members were stuffing themselves with chicken Parmesan. Small and comfortable, the room served as a place for Jasmine to relax and clear her head after services when she needed it.

"Your church is beautiful."

"Thanks."

"I'm sorry if I'm being intrusive. I tried so many times to call you. I've even stopped by your house throughout the week, but I haven't been able to reach you."

"I went away for the weekend."

"I've turned down the job," Monte said.

Jasmine froze. She wasn't expecting this. "Don't be silly. It's a wonderful opportunity."

"It's not the right opportunity."

"It's good money. You should take it." Her heart pounded in her chest. He'd come to tell her this because… Her fingers clutched her skirt and she tried to conceal her rising emotion.

"I don't need the money."

"Then why go on the interview?" Jasmine asked. She kept her tone as flat as possible. He'd sought her out tonight to tell her he planned to stay in Portsmouth. Could he—?

Monte glanced away for a moment. "I just wanted to further my career."

"Well, go further it." Jasmine tried to play it cool and hoped it worked. She couldn't allow him to see the glaze forming over her eyes. And she certainly didn't want him to see her cheeks flushed.

Monte met her gaze. "No, I'm staying here, Jasmine. I watched those boys last week. Tuesday. I can't believe it was that long ago. I listened to them express their love for you, and tears ran down my face. They made me realize I should have expressed to you something I'd been feeling for a long time. I love you."

Jasmine's body shook. She clasped her fists so hard that her nails dug into her palms. She looked into his eyes to see if she could gauge his sincerity. The moment she'd dreamed about had arrived. The man she craved wanted her and loved her.

"I love you, and I want to be with you," Monte continued. "I know I haven't been the most expressive guy, but I know what I'm feeling. I want to be with you. Just you. I'm going to stay here and continue the job I'm doing for now. I may find something else within the district, but I'm not going anywhere."

"I may be going away," Jasmine said. "I spent the long weekend in Florida looking into the program there." She fibbed, as she'd pretty much already made the decision to stay local. But she needed to know that he cared about her.

"That's fine," Monte said. "I'll wait for you. Flights from Portsmith are cheap. I'll visit you on weekends."

Jasmine turned away from him. She didn't need to face him—she could gauge his sincerity from his tone. His words couldn't have come at a worse time, for she wanted him, too. She hadn't fooled herself by running off to Florida. She'd done it out of hurt.

But could she really handle this now?

"I'm also putting my house up for sale."

Jasmines eyes widened. "Monte, stop—"

"No, not because I'm moving. Because I'm staying. I need to get out of the house. It's been little more than a shrine to Ellie and it's held me back. I'm still a young man. I can't hold on to that forever."

"Monte, you've given up so much already."

"No, not nearly enough. I need to give up that house. I've made the decision, and it's going to happen."

"I don't know what to say. I haven't really made up my mind about a college. I could just as easily go to Lafayette with you."

Monte's expression softened, then turned curious. He held her gaze for a moment before he spoke. "There is no Lafayette. I'm staying here. I went after that position for all the wrong reasons. I don't need the money. If I can't get a job like that locally—not necessarily in Portsmith but the surrounding area—then I don't want it."

He took her hand. "But that's sweet of you to make that kind of a sacrifice. It's just not necessary."

"It wasn't a sacrifice but an option. You still have options. We both do. I mean, as far as our careers."

"I'm not leaving you, Jasmine. You're the most amazing woman to come into my life. I love what we had together, and I want it to grow. I mean it. I know I said it before, but

I never expected to get that job. Besides, that's nothing compared to what I've got here."

Jasmine pulled her hand away from his and sat in one of the wicker chairs. She needed time. And if he meant what he said, he'd give her that time.

*Yeah, right.*

Time served as an excuse. She didn't need excuses. He'd been nothing short of wonderful to her. Encouraged her in her career move. Lifted her spirits when she'd been down. Helped her when he could by sharing contacts and pertinent information.

"What do you have here?" Jasmine asked.

Monte sat in the chair across from her.

"I've got my home, my career, my friends, my only nephew, and the woman I love."

"What makes you so sure you've got her?" Jasmine asked. The corners of her lips turned up in a smile.

Monte smiled. "Because you are the woman for me. That's how I know."

"Why me? What makes me so special?" Her voice grew softer.

Monte leaned closer to her. "One very important reason." He placed his hands on her shoulders. She did not flinch. "You are the only woman I have ever known in my life who doesn't nibble on her lower lip. Do you have any idea what it's like to kiss a calloused lip?"

Now, her smile grew broader.

"Jasmine, I mean it. You've helped me move on. Made me realize I can love again. In two years, I never came close to healing. Now, I've grieved. Cried for the first time. I need you."

"You cried?"

"Yes, when I saw those boys salute you."

Jasmine's eyes welled. She'd been so embarrassed at the time that the enormity of the gesture hadn't sunk in.

"They did a good job." Jasmine nodded. "And that did it for you?"

Monte sighed. "Yes. For two years, I hadn't found a way to grieve. Hadn't gone completely through the process. That was the last step."

"The last step is usually acceptance."

"Okay, so I did the steps out of order."

"Two years is a long time."

"That's what it took."

Jasmine placed her hand on Monte's arm. "I'm grateful I reached those boys. But how do I know I can duplicate that somewhere else?"

Monte smiled. "You don't know. It just happens. In different ways and at different times. Every class is different. That's public education."

Jasmine nodded. "Do other women really have calloused lips?"

Monte placed his lips against her soft, perfectly smooth lips. Jasmine's arms snaked around his neck and held the back of his head. She wasn't going anywhere. Monte was the man for her. She had known it for a long time, and trusted her instincts. The time had come for commitment and building a relationship. Florida had been an escape from the pain. She'd known all along she was being selfish. If he had a wonderful job opportunity, he should go for it. But he wasn't. He was staying here with her.

Together, they'd make it work. It had to. They'd met for a reason and had been reunited for a reason. She'd held back for too long. Now, Jasmine embraced living a full life. A new career and a man weren't impossible. She'd made it happen.

The moment she had seen him again at Brookhaven had signaled a new beginning. The awkwardness and miscommunication were things of the past. She'd put them behind her and move forward. Fighting her true passion had been futile. Monte had awakened something in her that had lain dormant.

She gazed at him, her body suddenly lightened of the burden of uncertainty. Nothing else mattered right now.

Jasmine's eyes welled from the rush of euphoria. The man she'd dreamed about at night was hers. The waves of warmth that overtook her every time she was near him did not betray her. Tears streamed down her cheek. Monte Davis would continue to be her man for richer, for poorer.

If you enjoyed Monte and Jasmine's story, please consider leaving a review on the retail site where you purchased it, or on Goodreads.

Monte and Jasmine also appear in the novelettes, *A Christmas Honeymoon* and *A Christmas Anniversary*.

# About the author

Jamie Jones writes interracial romance. Jamie spent nine years working as a public school teacher, and that provided the backdrop of Jamie's debut series, The Tempted Teachers Series. *Lesson Plans, Guided Practice,* and *Explicit Instruction* all take place within the framework of the public education system.

Now, Jamie is excited to introduce a new series: The Bennett Family Series. Jamie lives in Austin, Texas….where people are nice.

Visit my website at jamiejonesauthor.com

## Here is a brief excerpt from
### *Guided Practice*

She looked away. The magnitude of what she'd gotten herself into began to sink in. She'd left a cushy teaching job in a neighboring parish for this. Often, new gigs came with rocky starts, and she shouldn't let it get to her now. But it did.

"Did I say something wrong?"

Lara had her back to him. His strong, comforting hand squeezed her shoulder, and the tension melted. A wave of unfamiliar warmth slid through her body.

"I didn't mean to embarrass you. My classroom doesn't look any better."

*His touch.*

Lara relaxed, and she didn't want him to move his hand pressed against her shoulder. Of course, she couldn't stand there all day. They'd be missed. Lara turned to face Kelvin and placed her hand on his chest against one of his massive pectorals. It flexed, sending a shiver through her. She let out a slight gasp and her lips parted.

Kelvin moved closer, and his lips almost touched hers. His warm breath breezed against her. Her hand clenched against his chest, and her heart pounded even more urgently than her temples. The textbooks in his hand dropped to the floor.

She pushed away. "What time is it?"

He looked at his watch. "Five to nine."

"Shit! We need to be in the library at nine."

"You're right." Kelvin picked up the two textbooks he'd dropped. "I hope I didn't…"

"You didn't. Let's go. I have the impression Lady Hawthorne doesn't tolerate lateness."

Kelvin laughed.

Lara caught herself. "You didn't hear me say that."

They found their way out of the room and Lara locked the door. Her head spun. She couldn't believe she'd just allowed herself to be alone with a man. In fact, she couldn't remember the last time she had been in the same room with one.

# Also by Jamie Jones

*The Tempted Teachers Series*

*novels*
GUIDED PRACTICE (Book 2)
EXPLICIT INSTRUCTION (Book 3)

*novellas*
RESPONSE TO INTERVENTION (Book 4)
COMMON CORE (Book 5)
PROFESSIONAL DEVELOPMENT (Book 6)
BELL RINGERS (Books 4-6 in one volume)

*novelettes*
A HALLOWEEN TREAT
A HALLOWEEN TRICK
A CHRISTMAS HONEYMOON
A CHRISTMAS ANNIVERSARY
COMMON CORE: SUMMER SCHOOL
A THANKSGIVING GIFT
EARLY FINISHERS (all six novelettes in one volume)

*The Bennett Family Series*